Copyright

Fay's Wish
By
Dee Carver

Publication by Personalized Marketing Inc

Copyright © Dee Carol 2020
Editing: Cindy Wieczorek
Cover Art By: Cindy Wieczorek
https://PersonalizedMarketing.info
https://authordeeowens.blogspot.com

Dedication

First and foremost, thank you God for all the many blessings I have received. Remember, with God, your imagination can take you to the stars above.

To my kids who put up with my crazy hours writing, I love each and every one of you. To my mother who passed away in 2005— Mother, I miss you and I wish you could see this.

My father, for forcing me to express my thoughts, thanks Dad love you! To my Mom, thank you for all the support and giving me a new definition for 'a mother's love'. You didn't have to call me yours, but you did... Love and miss you each day. Hopefully my love for you came through in Shayla's love for her mother.

My loving and wonderful Grandparents, thank you for showing me responsibilities, you are dearly missed.

Cindy, thank you for taking time to help make my writing better with each red mark.

I would also like to say a special thank you to each one of you as you read Fay's Wish. Without you writing would not be the same.

God Bless,

Dee Carver

A GLIMPSE INTO WHAT IS TO COME
BY
SHAYLA GWENDOLYN DOMHNALL

Upon my Mother's death my Father, the King, was being forced to wed my Aunt Brigit. My worst adversary, Fearghus, was now my closest ally. How was it possible that the world I had known for over a hundred years no longer existed?

Fearghus had once been against everything my Mother and I had worked for. He wanted Fays to be allowed to go into the mortal's world once more and grow as a people again. I wanted the same thing, but for a different reason. I wanted the power, now lost to all Fay, returned. I would be crowned Queen after my Father's death. At one time, I foolishly thought that would be many centuries from now. Reality came crashing down around me this morning, when my mother faded from this world to the next.

Fearghus has agreed that I should go into the mortal's world, and upon my return be crowned Queen before my Father's passing. He said he believed it was time I no longer acted as the spoilt daughter, but the future of all Fay.

So here I stand, looking out at the ocean before me, knowing, if nothing else, my life would never be the same.

Chapter One

FAY ISLAND

The thunderous skies and shaking land had let me know how furious Anu, Mother Earth, and Lugh, Father Sun, were at the day's events. My Aunt was being crowned Queen this evening, as if my Mother's passing was nothing more than a distant thought. Stupid laws and traditions had forced me to not show the pain deep inside me.

Never more would Mother comfort me when I was ill, nor hold my hand when I was fearful. Never would she use magic to heal my many cuts and scrapes while learning something new. My Mother, my truest friend, was gone. None, but I, mourned her passing.

A soft downpour fell steadily, covering the tears that were flowing unchecked. I had refused to allow any to see my pain when she whispered her last words to me, and none saw them when they removed all trace of her existence from her deathbed.

No one saw my reaction when it was announced my Father, the King, would choose his new bride in only a few hours. Royalty have been forbidden to display their true feelings since my grandfather's rein when his Queen had left him for a mortal man. Since that fateful day, he decreed no one should know the truest thoughts and desires of their rulers. That nothing but death would separate the Royal Couple and that all Fay after him would have to choose a new mate before the sun rose on another day.

Now, I was expected to act as though nothing untoward was happening as a new Queen was chosen to replace my Mother. My Father had yet to shed a tear over her passing.

"Oh Mother, I miss you so!" The words ripped from my very soul.

"Princess Shayla, your presence is requested inside," Jacques, or as I nicknamed him Jack, said softly behind me. Of all the Guards I knew, Jack had loved my mother the most. I sensed his pain at interrupting my grief over her death. "I shall be in momentarily. I have something to do first." I tried not to show the tears. I did not know how they would affect him.

He had taken a silk-cloth from his pocket and wiped them away. "A true Lady should never have to dry her own tears. Your mother, Queen Gwendolyn, once told this to me as she wiped my own mother's tears at my Father's passing. I do not know if it was what I saw in her eyes that day, or in the tender movement of her actions, but it has been with me since."

I knew the tenderness he spoke of and nodded my head in understanding. Royals were never allowed to show pain for the loss of anyone. To wipe the face of a commoner would have been unthinkable.

"Yes. There will never be anyone as kind or considerate as my mother."

As my body shook, I placed my hand on Jack's arm and let him lead me. I knew why I had been summoned. My Father had chosen his new bride and I was to witness the ceremony.

In rebellion, I chose to wear the deepest blue I could find. It was as close as I could get to black. Fays are forbidden such desolate colors. We are the celebration of Anu, and should always show such, but I was tired of hiding my true self from others, tired of trying to be something I was not. Perfect.

Once inside the throne room, very few of the Fay had shown any sympathy for my forced presence. If any had grieved at all, no one would suspect it. All the faces had been void of any feelings. Most of them seemed disappointed in the fact I had any feelings left at all. I was resolved to no longer blend in the fold, but to stand out among the masses.

A single tear trickled down my cheek. Before, I would have discretely whipped it away, but now I would allow that tear to fall as it may. Once I refused to wipe the first, many fell freely, as though I no longer had control over my own emotions.

Maybe I hadn't, but I was more truthful with myself in that moment, than I had ever been in my life.

"Ah how good of you to join us, Cousin. I hope our traditions do not trouble you. Your Father has decided to allow the council to choose his new bride. I cannot wait to hear their decision."

Aidan's voice grated upon my skin; his every word filled with malice. I had tensed for the killing blow. The sarcasm of his reminder of Fay traditions, instilled in me since birth, had been a strike against me.

Contempt struck each syllable I spoke. "Oh, fear not, Aidan. I am sure your ears are more than large enough to hear what they have to say."

Aidan was an embarrassment. Teased, he despised the length of his ears since childhood. Some of the Fay said they made up for lack of wings, a trait passed down in his family for years. It was a reminder of their disgrace. That one of their line had disobeyed the law or fallen from grace and allowed a human into their lineage.

"Enough!" Father's voice carried from his position on the throne. "The council is ready to speak and does not wish to listen to childish bickering."

I had finally noticed the Queen's throne had been placed in the center of the room on a floating platform, as though whoever sat in it was not good enough until they had wed the King. It would stay in that position until a Queen was chosen and the wedding complete. Sadly, both a King and Queen were needed to keep the island safe. Their magic combined with all of Fay allowed them to not only cloak our Island but to move it as well.

"Yes," Fearghus, the oldest Elder commanded as he glared at me. "Since the King has shown no interest in choosing his own bride, the Council has chosen for him. Your Aunt Brigit will become the new Queen. As she and her kin are related by marriage only, the Gods should grace the union. We have made our decision, and it shall stand from this moment forward."

I watched in disbelief as the Elders left the throne room in preparation for the night's ceremony.

My Aunt Brigit was to become my stepmother? I turned in time to see a smirk of determination fall from Aunt Brigit's face. Turning toward my Father, I saw why. He had waited too long to choose his own bride and could not go against the Elder's rule. I watched the disgust burn in his gray eyes, and I knew no child would come of their union.

Aunt Brigit sped hastily from the room as I went to Father's side.

"Shayla, you look so much like your Mother, it almost hurts to gaze upon your beautiful face. Having you helps ease my pain. I miss her more than you could know. I realize you are upset by the Elders' decision, as am I, but we do not have a choice in this. I must take Brigit for my bride, and you must accept her as your Queen. You must also submit to Aidan being your brother for now."

My Father's face was emotionless, but in their shiny depths, his eyes held the pain he was going through.

"Father, can I ask you something?" I had spoken softly so none would overhear us.

"What is it, Shayla? What's the matter?"

"Why did you allow the council to choose for you? I miss Mother greatly, and marriage to Aunt Brigit would have torn her apart. Why not choose an ally or friend?"

"Your Mother and I promised on our wedding day, we would never choose to marry another if one of us died without the other. A testament to our love, we had this written in our vows. I must admit, I was hoping the council would have chosen someone other than your Aunt. But fate has other plans."

"Fate, Father? I have never heard you speak of your own fate before."

"I am not speaking of my own fate, daughter. I speak of the fate of all Fay. Your Mother was right. We are dying as a people. I just wish I had told her when she was still with us. She had been right, and now it is too late."

One tear slipped down his face. I knew then, though my loss was great, his was terrible. Witnessing the love my Father would carry forever for my Mother, I thought of what she had told me.

"What is wrong Shayla," Father asked. "Why do you now look so sad?"

I told him what Mother had wished for.

"My sweet, sweet daughter. How I shall miss you the most. I am sorry to leave you this way and have only one wish left in me. I shall share it with you."

"What is it, Mother? What do you wish of me?"

"I ask that you watch after your Father and yourself. My wish, however, is for you. I wish for you to find love, my daughter, and not just any love, but a love like your Father's and mine. A love greater than all things and all time. A love to keep you warm on a cold night, to give you light in the bitter darkness, to fill your body and soul when you feel there is no joy left to be had. Your heart's desire, your deepest secret, your sleeping mind's cry, your true love. When you find your true love, let nothing, or no one stand in your way. Let the Gods themselves guide and protect it, while the Goddesses nurture it and tend it, until it overcomes anything and anyone around you. That is the wish, and the last thing I ask. A great love for you, my daughter, greater than any man or woman has ever known."

I then told my Father how I felt. "I cannot fulfill her wish. I have searched among the Fay, and none yet call to me, to see the woman behind the Crown. None know my deepest desires, my darkest secrets, or the things that frighten me most. Not one Fay, not ever."

"I have wondered what she said to you. Shayla, you must understand. We did not love each other when we met. It was something precious that has grown over time. You also know, love is not a requirement of a good marriage. Few are ever lucky enough to have love enter their lives, let alone a love that lasts.

We will talk about this and many other things tomorrow, but for now, as much as we would prefer not to, we must prepare for the wedding."

I placed my hand on his arm and allowed him to lead me to my rooms. When we reached the door, he placed a kiss on my forehead. As he made his way down the hall, I knew I must be by his side tonight. We needed each other more than ever before.

With a deep sigh, I went into my rooms and prepared for the ceremony.

Chapter Two

THE FAVOR

As I stood looking at my reflection in the mirror, a brisk knock sounded at the door. Expecting Father, I put a smile on my face to receive him. The smile fell when I opened the door and saw Aidan standing there.

"Now Cousin...or should I say...sister." Aidan seemed to devour the word. "Is this any way to treat a member of your family? Are you going to invite me in? No? Then you will take my arm, so I may escort you to the wedding."

"Do not think you shall be allowed to order me around," I spat at him. "It's no matter our parents will marry, we will never be more than what we are now."

"And what is that, my sweet sister?"

"Enemies!" I hissed.

Laughter rumbled from his chest. "Enemies? Maybe. After tonight we will be much more. Much, much more. Who knows just how close we shall become in the future. Now, shall we go?"

I shook as Aiden's arm extended in front of me and wondered how much time there was until the ceremony started.

"Princess Shayla. I was just coming to fetch you." From down the hall, Jack hurried toward us wearing his dress uniform.

The blaze in his eyes, barely held in check, sent shivers down my spine. I realized he would kill Aidan if he could. His timing evoked a satisfied smile on both our faces.

"Just one moment, Jack. Let me fetch my shawl."

"No!" Aiden shrieked. "I came to escort my cousin to our parents wedding. I shall be the one to take her, not you."

"I am sure the Princess greatly appreciates the offer, but King Domhnall commanded me to bring her to his side. You do not want me to disobey the King, do you?"

"No. I do not wish you to disobey an order from the King." Aiden spun toward me. "I shall see you later, my dear." He stormed away, but I knew he would find a way to make us both pay for the insult.

Jack stood patiently. Placing my hand on his arm, I pulled him closer than I needed. I may never love him, but I will always respect him.

"Tell me truthfully. Did Father send you to fetch me?"

"Truthfully, I must confess. He asked me only to send you to the Gardens for a meeting. He wishes to ask a favor in private." Jack had the grace to look embarrassed for a moment.

"Do not feel guilty for lying, for you did not. You did as commanded." I started to pull my arm away but stopped. "Do you now offer an escort for duty, or for friendship?"

"Both. I shall always be loyal to you, Princess, but also because you will always mean more to me than just my future Queen."

His statement forced me to pause, and I turned my head to look up into his eyes. He stood a foot taller than I. It was then, that I noticed the growing love for me in his eyes. The love came through every movement, or lack of. For the first time, I understood. He had cherished me, and not my Mother.

"Ah, Jack. You will always be more to me than a subject of my future people. You have meant more to me than I can ever say, but..." I had not been sure how to explain I could never love him.

"I understand you shall never love me, but it will not change the way I feel about you. Knowing you feel even remotely for me, is more than enough." Jack cleared his throat. "You and your Father have a very long night ahead of you. Shall we?"

I nodded my head and fell into step beside him. The muscles of his arm flexed beneath my fingertips.

The tension of our brief talk carried in each step we took, but I could not think of a way to fix it.

Jack left me standing at the entrance to the Garden. There, Father stood in the center waiting for me. No longer trying to find a way to repair the drift in my friendship with Jack, I focused on why I was here. It was not the King needing a Princess, but a Father needing his Daughter.

"Come, I must ask a great favor of you, and wish to know your answer in private."

I walked to him. He took my hand gently, before lowering his head.

"Father, what is it? You can ask anything you wish of me; you know that."

He looked up with hope in his eyes. "You are aware, a member of the groom's family stands beside him to represent the blessing and support of the union. I wish you to stand beside me tonight. Not many from my family are alive, but none means more to me than you. I realize you feel the same, as I do, about this union, but that is not why I am asking you to do this for me. I wish you to support and trust me, whatever happens tonight. Standing at my side will show it."

"I will always support you. Of course, I shall stand by your side. May I ask what else is going to take place tonight?"

"Thank you, Shayla. I wish I could say, but I am afraid I must ask you to wait as everyone else. Now...may I escort my lovely Daughter, the Princess of Fay to the ceremony?"

"Yes Father, King of Fay. Know that whatever decision you make, I have complete faith in you."

We walked slowly, but more surely than ever before, to the Moon Chamber, where all of Fay were waiting.

Chapter Three

WEDDING AND DECREE

As I stood beside my father, I wondered what he might do or say. I looked around the room, now lit by the shimmering moon. It was significant. Something was going to happen. Something on a life altering scale.

I turned to watch Aunt Brigit and Cousin Aidan walk toward us, reflections of triumph and greed in their pale, silvery eyes. For many years, they coveted father's throne. I had not realized how much until right then, and I began to wonder about Aidan's earlier words. *What made him think we would become closer? What did they have up their sleeves?*

The ceremony was simple. It required the joining of hands with a magical rope constructed of gold twine and one silver thread running through it. The Moon Goddess, Cerridwen, had cursed the thread, and the curse was as fresh as the day it was cast. If any broke their vow of fidelity, they lost their powers and lived out their days in shame. Even marriages, such as the one between my father and Aunt Brigit, must be sacred and faithful until the day one or both died.

Once Father and Aunt Brigit's wrists were bound, they turned to the elders, and then to the statues of Anu, Lugh, and Cerridwen, showing their respect. As one, they turned to us, before walking down the aisle and leading everyone from the room. An ominous cloud covered the moon as we entered the Throne Room, and the Deities did not appear. It foretold no blessing of this union.

Yet, in most royal marriages, the more powerful or original would be the absolute ruler. As others before him, my Grandfather chose his new bride and retained his authority. I had hoped the same applied now, but the Elders made the choice, and nothing was certain.

Father spoke. "Before we take our place on the throne as King and Queen of Fay, I have a decree to make. The law forbidding Fay from leaving the island is lifted for Princess Shayla and Jack of the Guard. She is to leave the island on a quest for her true power. If she finds it, then upon her return, she will become Queen. Jack is to go with her to protect and help in her quest. Jack has also requested that he be considered as her future groom and King of Fay. I believe this to be a good idea, and he has my blessings. If Shayla is successful, the law forbidding Fay to leave our lands shall be lifted. We may finish the ceremony and crown Shayla as the new Queen."

The silence was deafening. Not a single Fay moved, and a few looked as though they were holding their breaths. I could hardly believe it. Everything my mother strove for had been granted on the day of her death. The Fay's future now fell on my shoulders, but was I strong enough to support my duty?

Centuries ago, we were commanded to go on a quest for our true power. After a journey of self-discovery, and seeing inside our hearts, this power would emerge. When humans began hunting the Fay for influence and immortality, it became forbidden to leave.

It was my Grandfather who proclaimed the ban. He lost his much-loved first wife to humans, and for as long as the Fay have existed, both King and Queen must have someone to rule by their side. When a ruler refuses his duties, the Elders have the right to command the Laws be followed or remove them from the throne. After searching for months, my Grandfather was ordered to choose a new bride. His own law had come back on him.

My own Mother was not old enough to wed or rule then. Grandfather admitted his ban unfair and rash but would not do away with it. Some feared it would eventually cost the Fay all their powers. He said the loss of Fay lives would be more devastating than the loss of magic itself.

We still possessed some magic, but the great power existed no more. Mother tried to have the ban abolished. She felt, as others did, that we lost our glory as well. She saw each generation with less magic and life, than the ones before. The Elders themselves are dying at an earlier age.

I believe the most painful loss though was that the females could no longer conceive after three hundred years. I believed their loss of fertility meant we were doomed. We only conceived once, every one hundred years now, and not all the children survived. I feared one day, Fay would not be able to give birth at all.

We as a people were dying.

I turned to where Jack stood and saw he had wanted to tell me of his request but had been afraid to. I felt grief, but not anger toward him. I knew there was no way we could ever wed.

"How can you do this, Domhnall?" Aunt Brigit demanded.

"We are just wed, and already you take the crown from my head. I will not stand by and allow you to do this. I say to the Elders, if the Princess fails, then upon her return, she is to wed my son, Aidan. She should also take with her another besides Jack, since he has shown interest in her as a bride. We do not want a child to be conceived during this quest. All Fay know the tale. We are more fertile in the mortal realm. So, I ask you, Elders. Do you grant my request and see my reasoning behind it?"

I knew why they had been so smug. Brigit had found out my fathers' plans and had made her own. It also explained Aidan's actions and words. *When had Father decided this?* Was this what he had wanted to talk to my mother about for the past few weeks, and never had the time? Her death had changed my life, some for the better, but most of it could not be any worse than a nightmare conjured on my own.

"Who would you suggest, Queen Brigit?" Fearghus inquired from his place near the two thrones.

"My son perhaps, but no. I think a female companion would serve best in this journey someone who is not already wed, and not too young or old. Why not Aine? She has just reached the marriageable age. As she is named after a Great Goddess, she will be the epitome of grace and virtue." Brigit smiled sweetly to the Elders but kept her eye on Fearghus.

"I agree with our Queen. If the Princess is to go on this journey, then she will be accompanied by both."

The Elders nodded heads in agreement, before turning and leaving the room.

I kept my eyes adverted as Aidan and I loosened the bonds from Father and Brigit's wrists. Though we had not yet crowned Brigit as our new Queen, Fearghus declaring so in front of everyone, made her so. Only an Elder, or a God or Goddess, could decree it with words. It was another tradition that should be abolished.

I could not understand it. Fearghus had always been against Mother and reversing the law. Now, he was agreeing to it. If I failed, I would be forced to wed Aidan. Fearghus seemed adamant that our two families be joined. I knew part of it was for mortal blood. He had been championing Fay with human blood, since his return from their world.

Mother told me of his venture into their world to save Grandfather's bride. I did not know fully what happened. It, like many other tales of the Fay, is forgotten or forbidden. I yet wonder, what could have occurred to change him so. Maybe, while I looked for my own power, I could find out what happened.

I looked up to see my father before me. Alone.

"You are not angry with my decision are you, Shayla? I know it has been a long time coming, but the moment had not seemed right until now."

"No, I am not angry. I only wish Mother had been alive to witness it."

"I'm glad you approve, but that is not what I wish to talk about. I speak of your betrothal to Jack. You are more than old enough to wed. You have long passed your one-hundredth birthday."

"Yes, Father, but I am only one hundred and thirty this year. I hardly think that is too old. I still have many more years, before I need to worry about being too old to marry or plan a family. Is this why you changed the law? So, I would not be angry at you for deciding that I needed to marry?"

"No, the law should have been changed long ago. My marriage to Brigit has only hastened my decision. I do not want her on the throne long enough to cause any damage to our people. I would have stepped down for you, if I could have. But the law clearly states you must be married first. The only other way is my death, but you would have to marry the moment you were crowned. This way you can rectify a terrible mistake, and end that which needs ending. It will also give you a chance to get better acquainted with Jack."

I could not help the confusion or hurt from seeping into my words. "You are saying you did this, so I can take my place on the throne without fear of

Aidan? But, why Jack? I thought you understood how I felt."

"I do understand your need for love, but you have said there is no love in you for any Fay. This is the only way I know to fix this. If I stepped down, the Elders would give you to Aidan, and this is another thing we cannot allow. I will have a hard-enough time dealing with Brigit and her schemes."

"As long as you and Brigit are wed, then Aidan cannot convince the council to force a union."

"That is true, but if the vows of my marriage were broken, then it could happen. Is the idea of marrying Jack so terrible, you would be willing to risk spending your life with Aidan?"

"No. Jack is a good man, though I believe he deserves more than I could ever give him. Why is Fearghus trying so hard to unite our families? He cared for Mother, even though they disagreed on many things. We both know she would have fought this."

"I am not sure; I only know he has been this way since he returned to us." He smiled. "Tomorrow will be a big day for you. I think we should both rest."

"Tomorrow? Do you mean I should leave so soon?"

"Yes. The sooner you leave, the faster you will return to me."

I allowed him to lead me to the Gardens, where I asked him to go on without me.

"Are you sure, Shayla? I can wait with you if you want me to."

"No. I will be fine."

Chapter Four
THE FIRST KISS

As I entered the garden, the smell of succulent roses flowed through my body, while the path itself was soothing with vibrant green and deep red stones. Gliding softly over the smooth stones, I headed for the waterfalls, sighing in pleasure as the soft moss lining it caressed and soothed my feet and heart. In all of Fay Island, this was my sanctuary. A place I could be myself, forget royal burdens and courtly duties. When I was younger, I often found myself drawn here to search for my perfect mate.

In the center of the Garden, a mist was gathering against the steep rocks. Staring down I contemplated the brilliance flowing beneath the spray as it cast a shimmering silver hue in its depths. The sound of chimes filled the air as the falls began to play a sweet melody all of their own.

"They say when the water is such color, magic is trying to reach out to a Fay," Aine said.

I turned and took in her beauty. As always, she was hidden behind a garment of deep red, this time however the hood draping her face was pulled back. I was struck at the mane of red hair flowing around her body; it reminded me of silk caressing the radiant face now in full view.

As I contemplated Aine, I could not understand why she hid behind the red shroud. Her beauty was astounding. "If the water changed for one Fay, then who is it? You and I are the only ones here."

"It is waiting to receive you. I have been here for some time, and the water did not change until you arrived."

The look of poise on her face made me wonder if she might be right. I turned toward the water, sensing it call to me, beckoning me to step in.

I do not know whether it was Aine's faith, or the water itself, but I waded in before I could stop to think. The water swirled around my body, stroking each curve with an intimate caress. I expected it to be cooler as I waded further in, but instead, it grew hot. Aine had been right. The water was responding to my touch, my intimate power. I was sure of it. Since my birth, there had not been a gift of magic such as this given. For whatever reason, I was to receive an old and precious gift.

"Do not be frightened, Princess, let the water carry you, comfort you, love you. Let it give you it's offering in great joy. Know that, of the entire Fay, you are the one to receive a blessing from it."

Aine's words made sense. The water's magic wanted to love me, caressing my body with its essence, giving me the bounty, it was. It was now up to me to love it in return.

Taking her words and my thoughts to heart, I closed my eyes and opened my arms. The water pushed against my thighs, and I lifted my feet in response. Cradling me in lover's arms, the water held my head above itself, before carrying me into its depth. Not once did I panic. I trusted the water as though it were my lover. The magic of the moment provided all I needed to survive. Opening my eyes, the water radiated silvery magic and faded to midnight blue, pulsating with resilient energy. Part of my mind screamed of the danger surrounding me, but my heart could only rejoice.

At that moment, I saw him. His eyes were the deepest blue I had ever seen, with silver flecks shooting out from the center of it, the same vividness as the water surrounding us. A ring of forest green surrounded the blue. The coal black hair made his creamy skin rich. Everything about him left no doubt to any of my senses. My whole body vibrated. From his chiseled features, to his broad shoulders, he was everything I had ever dared dream. He emanated male. I could only guess at his height, but he seemed taller than life to me.

My enchantment had caught me off guard. His height compared to a male Fay in his prime, and I wondered why I had never met him before. In reaction to my query, his surroundings changed from an island forest to a small town. The buildings were constructed of a wood I knew had not been made by Fay, but by man.

My heart faltered. He was human. Nothing was to come from these feelings building deep inside of me.

Fay have been forbidden to mate with humans, and the few half-bloods left were either from before my Grandfather's rule, or descendants of those who had ventured into the mortal's world.

The water grew intense. Had I said or done something to upset the magic? The image of the man clarified again. He was in the very water with me. From within, I could not stop the heat from rising, as I watched our bodies begin to entwine with each other. Each kiss he placed upon my skin burst like sunlight through the mists.

My breasts lifted to his lips as the climax began to grow in my abdomen and move lower. My entire body became heavy with a need I had not felt before.

With each powerful stroke inside me, my skin grew hotter. It echoed the inferno surrounding us. I had only heard of such impulsive things happening between the Gods and Goddesses. When our bodies peaked, his grip told me he felt each sensation I did.

I only hoped he thought he was dreaming, or I would begin to fear for his mind. According to tales from the Elders, humans no longer believed in the Fay, and only a few believed that magic existed at all. Most of those thought magic evil.

He reached out. Not toward my image, but to me, seeing through the mist as I had. The steel in his eyes concerned and frightened me. At first, confusion and doubt overcame him. Then, an unmistakable desire to possess me emerged.

The water started to swirl. My lover disappeared, his last visage a promise. If I ever met him, he would master all of me to be had.

The water became lighter and cooler to my skin. As I rose to the top and emerged, my surroundings became airy once more. I was not sure how deep I had gone, but without the magic, I'm sure I would have drowned.

"Princess!" Aine cried. "Are you all right? The water became so murky, I could not see you at all!"

"There is no need to worry. All is well."

Jack stood beside my Father and Aine. His face normally filled with concern, now held a spark of lust. Father's face was furrowed with anger. Anger I had not seen for a long time, and that grew with each passing second.

Seeing their stares, I feared I knew what had put such looks on their faces. I gazed down at my body. The plastered gown left nothing of me to the imagination. I attempted to hide myself, when another voice sent chills down my spine.

"Why cover yourself now? We have already seen what your clothes have once hidden from us. I wondered why you dressed so. Now, I know. You are exquisite. Come, Cousin. Embrace your heritage. Do not hide your body in shame. Display it for all to see as a Princess of Fay should. Remove your ruined gown. Let the Gods see what they have created."

Aidan spoke deeply, but his lust was edged with the kind of taint no woman would want directed at her. He meant to have me. No matter what I, or anyone else, chose.

"Remember to whom you speak," Jack responded icily.

"You may be Prince by marriage, but she is Princess by birth and a higher rank than you."

"Enough! Magic has happened here. I think it is more important than what my daughter chooses to wear. Aine, can you tell me what has happened?"

"Yes," Aine's voice trembled softly.

I wondered if it was from fear of my Father, or from wonder at what had happened.

"The water chose to share with her. What it chose to share exactly, I do not know."

"You say it wanted to share with her, what did it give her?"

"I do not know, Majesty. I am not even sure Princess Shayla can tell you."

Father turned to me. "Do you know?"

"No, Father. I am sorry. The water held me in its care and shared power with me, but I do not know to what extent."

"Is there more?"

I thought about my answer. I knew I could not lie to him, but I did not wish to tell it all, either. "I had a vision of the human world. Why, I do not know."

"I believe I know the answer to that," Aine murmured.

"Speak! Do not fear my reaction."

Father never showed his rule with such force, but today it seemed he would brook no provocation.

"I believe the Gods were sending their blessing for the Princess' journey. I also believe they feel this has been a long time coming."

"Do you feel the same?" Fearghus asked me, his voice incredulous. "Do you think it is past time?"

I wondered with some disgust; how many people had witnessed my private moment. "Yes."

"It is decided, then. You shall leave on the morrow. I suggest the three of you rest and only pack for a few days. Anything you need, you can purchase on the way."

Fearghus shook his head as he followed Father out of the garden.

"I will escort the Princess to her room," Aine said, gone was the sound of fear and replaced with something new. The tone of her voice brought no refusal from either Jack or Aidan.

Once we were at my door, Aine motioned me inside. "I need to speak to you in private, Princess."

"Yes?"

"I do not know what happened in the water, but I do know it was for a reason. There was a man involved. He will play a large role in your destiny. You do not have to explain to me what happened, but I fear everyone knows it was intimate. There is one more thing. I saw the way your cousin looked at you. You must be careful of him and avoid his advances at all cost. He must not succeed in his plans of seduction."

"Have no fear, Aine. My cousin shall know my blade before he knows my body. We must do as we were bid and prepare ourselves for the morrow."

"Yes. Princess Shayla? With only a fortnight till Yule, do you think it is wise to leave now?"

I thought for a moment. Yule was once a time of great celebration and powerful magic. Now it only reminded us of things gone by and another day during the winter season. "We have no choice. I have no choice."

When Aine was gone, I carefully packed a few things and prepared for the next day.

Chapter Five
THE FIRST DREAM

"Who are you?"

"Shayla."

"Shayla. I like it. What does it mean?"

I puzzled a moment over the question, deciding the man from the pool would either laugh, or would not. Being mortal, he may think it a jest. "Fay Palace."

"It suits you. You can only be magic. Are you real?"

"As much as you are."

"I'm sorry to hear that. I would prefer magic."

"Why?"

"I'm dying." His voice held no remorse, only distant logic.

With a will of its own, my voice deepened. "Why? Are you hurt? Or is it just your time?" Even though his whimsy believed I was a dream, I knew differently. I might not be able to do much, but there was always a chance.

"I'm not hurt. I turned thirty last year and no male in my family has lived past thirty. I will pass away on the eve of my next birthday."

"I am sorry to hear it. Is it some type of curse placed on your family?" I did not know him, but the thought of his death caused a brutal piercing in my gut.

"Curse? Yeah, I guess you could say that. It is an old and long story. Maybe I will tell you about it some other time. Can I ask you something?"

"Anything." I did not know why, but I could hide nothing.

"If you're real, and I'm real, how is right now even possible?"

"Fate. The Gods and Goddesses have decided we should meet, and this is the only way."

"Okay, say you're right. Why can't we meet for real?"

"I do not know where you are, but it is worlds apart. We can never be together in the real world."

"That's pretty final. Haven't you heard of airplanes? They fly all over the world."

"I am sorry, you do not understand. Anything more would result in your death. My people are not cruel, but we no longer have tolerance for humans. Our mating would be a death sentence."

"Oh, I get it. I'm good enough to have unworldly sex with, but not good enough to arouse in real life. Cold, lady. Really, cold." He turned and walked away.

"Wait! You never told me your name."

"No, I didn't, and I don't plan to, either. You can just blow off."

I flinched. "Wait! Please. I am sorry. I do not make the rules, I just live by them."

"What do you mean 'just live by them'?" He did not turn, but at least stopped walking away from me. "The real world doesn't follow out-of-date rules. Where are you from?"

"A place you've never heard of. Where rules of the old still apply. You may not wish to believe it, but I am a Princess and have more rules to follow than most."

"A dream Princess, from a dream world, then. What about then? Or now? Why give me my deepest desire, only to take it away?"

"That is for the Gods to know and for us to find out. Just accept this gift for what it is. The last of my people to break the law of mating with a mortal was punished, and the mate killed."

"Gods! Mate! As in what we did?"

I could only nod. Who was he that he would refer to the 'Gods' as I had? Was I wrong, was he Fay?

"Are you all right? You seem upset or scared."

The tenderness in his voice struck like a harp string and brought tears to my eyes. "I am fine, but you must understand we can never go any farther. We must never meet." I suspected, unless we accidentally ran into each other on my journey, all this worry meant very little. But his beliefs still filled me with concern.

"Well, if this is all we can ever have, I guess we should make the best of it. My name is Kyle."

"Hello, Kyle." *Now why did I say that?* "I am sorry. It is a bit trivial to say hello now."

"No. Never. I love hearing you say it. From now on, I want you to say it each time we meet."

He was no longer facing away from me, but relaxed, in a small pool of water. "I am in a hidden pool near my home. Care to join me?"

"If you'd like." I could not believe how his request caused my chest to swell. I hesitated. "I can see some of what is around you, but not exactly where you are."

"What do you see now?"

He was still in the pool of water. I was struck with a horrible idea. "I need to ask you a couple things first."

"Anything, sweetheart."

"Can you see where I am now?"

"You are lying on a huge bed made of silver and wood."

It was as I feared. He could see what was around me. "You mention relaxing, right? Are you asleep, dreaming your bath, or awake?"

"Awake. Aren't you?"

"No. I am asleep. We must be very careful. If my people knew you could see where I am, they would punish me and hunt you down."

"You keep speaking of your people. Just who and what are they?"

"I cannot reveal that, but I am a true Princess. I would like to join you, but it is best I do not. The first time we met, what happened to you? Can you explain how you got there, and what happened after?"

"Sure. I was walking through the woods when I saw you under a canopy of trees. You opened your arms to me, and I wanted nothing more than to touch you. The next thing I knew, we were in dark blue water that glowed. After, when I was back in the forest, my clothes were wet and lying on the ground beside me." He paused. "What are you thinking?"

"We are in serious trouble. I will join you in the water, but only for a moment, then I must go. I promise to try and return though. I need to know something, and the only way is when I am awake."

"You make a promise of seeing me again?"

"I do not think either of us could stop, even if we wanted." I did not want to stop. If not for his life being forfeit, I would stay with him as long as the Gods allowed.

"Come and tell me goodbye, then."

I crossed over to him, letting the water soak through my gown, and did what I desired to since we'd first met. Whispering leaning over him, I caressed the sides of his face, and brushed my lips against his mouth. His lips were warmer, fuller, and more real than I ever imagined. He was made for me. Everything I ever wanted in a mate, kept inside my dreams where we could not be hurt.

I jerked away and turned, wishing to end the dream. Awake in my room, I guessed right. My gown was soaked. What we had done affected both physical worlds. This was a gift and a curse, and there would be repercussions. I had everything I could want, but was in the gravest danger of my life.

Chapter Six
LEAVING FAY ISLAND

I met my father and the others at the gates to our city. He had decided we would be safe leaving by boat. The portal was quick, but there was no guarantee a human would not see.

He pointed to a pocket deep inside the small purse I would carry. "I have concealed currency for you, but if there is a need for more, there are accounts set up all through Scotland that you can draw money out of. When you return, you will have to use magic to find the island.

Be careful. Do not let anyone see, or the Gods forbid, follow. Be swift in your return, Daughter. We shall miss you." Father embraced me, then turned to the others. "Take care of yourself and the women, Jack. Aine, guide her as best you can. She may need your sight. I am counting on you both." Father kissed my forehead and stepped away.

"Yes, Aine. Guard her virtue well. I do not wish to have my bride pregnant with another man's babe," Aidan yelled from above us.

One of these days, he is going to push me too far and I will hurt him. I ignored Aidan and turned to Father and Fearghus. "Take care yourself. I shall miss you. Fearghus, I hope to restore your faith in me, and bring back my true power."

"We shall see, Princess. When you arrive in Ireland, you will take a plane to Inverness, Scotland. A man will be waiting for you. He does not know your true self, of course. He believes you to be a noblewoman, so behave as such."

"Yes, Fearghus. I shall not embarrass you or my people. How will we know him?"

"His name is Kyle, and he will carry a miniature of the Goddess Morrigan. Ask to see it before you follow him."

I nodded. *Wait was it possible? Kyle? It could not be him.* Fearghus frowned as he walked away. Not wanting any other surprises, I marched down to the pier and stepped into the boat.

The motorboat was sleek with a powerful engine in the stern. I overheard it had been purchased for speed and maneuverability, not to spend time in. It looked new and unused. Who had bought it, and how, if we are now not allowed contact with the mortal realm?

Father blessed us, as we cast off. "The island will be in the same spot for a fortnight. Good luck, Shayla. May the Gods be with you."

It only took a couple of hours to reach Ireland. Father and Aunt Brigit must have moved Fay Island as close as they dared, while we slept. None of us spoke. Even the usually garrulous guards chose to remain silent. I had plenty of time to think about Kyle, but I hoped the Gods were not so cruel. *Would he be waiting for us at the airport? How would he react?* I yearn for him more than anyone or anything, but his life is more precious than any of that.

The motorboat banked and we got out.

"Now that we are alone, will you tell me why you were so stunned over the man we will meet?" Jack's voice vibrated with the frustration I felt. Maybe he knew something I did not. Being 250 should have benefits.

"It was nothing. I was surprised Fearghus hired a human male is all. And the fact he also wishes me to marry Aidan. I thought it very strange for him to offer help." It may not be the whole truth, but close enough.

Even if I believed Fearghus would set me up to fail, I didn't think any of us would be hurt. I could not return home without the power. The future I had waiting with Aidan was more than enough incentive.

"I agree we should not trust this human. Fearghus may have arranged for him to cause your failure."

Jack's mouth was set. He would make it harder than necessary.

Aine only shrugged. "I suggest we get to our plane. We do not wish to keep our guide waiting."

The anger coming from her confused me.

"Yes. Let us be done with this." Jack responded. "The sooner we meet, the faster we can be rid of him."

Oh, yes. They are going to argue. Jack was going to make this as hard as possible. And Aine was upset at Jack.

"I believe we should not be too hasty in our actions against this man. If we do not use his services, then he may tell Fearghus. That may end up hurting the Princess in the long run. Fearghus is already angry at her, so why give him any more reason to be?"

"What did I say? I am only voicing what we are all thinking. Fearghus hired him. It would be easy for him to stop the Princess from finding her power. He wishes for her to fail, so why not set her up?"

I walked away, picking a way through the rocks. "Aine is right. We should wait and see." I did not care if they agreed or not. This journey was going to be hard enough without them arguing the whole trip.

The eight-seater held two crew and six passengers. We had to duck getting inside, and I was not fond of small places. The excursion would only take a couple of hours, but it would seem an eternity. *How could I find power in this world, in this tiny craft?*

Chapter Seven

COMING FACE TO FACE

As the plane lifted, I wondered for a second time, how my Father and Fearghus managed to schedule our trip. They must have used all the contacts the Fay knew in the human world. And I yet wondered, if all contact had been broken with humans, how we were staying current with their lives and history. Who would they be in touch with to plan all this in such a short time?

Some of us knew more than others. I remember Fearghus was once questioned about the Elder's vast knowledge of the human world. The reply was orderly. "We own a great deal of property there. We must keep track of it using various resources."

I had not believed the excuse then, and really did not believe it now. How could they know so much and not have an unknown motive? Why the curiosity?

At the airport, Jack, Aine and I took our luggage from the crew. I hoped...no, I prayed the man we were to meet was not my Kyle. I did not want to see his striking face coming toward me and breaking my heart.

The Gods however had their own agenda. He stood, straight as an island tree, eyes wide. My mind numbed and turned to fear for both of our lives, while realization and a look of triumph emerged across his face. I stepped backwards as he strode with intent to us. To me.

"Kyle?" Aine asked, coming up beside me.

"Yes ma'am. You must be my noble guests. I believe I am to show you this." His voice, a melody.

The Gods were in full force. In his hand he held the miniature of the Goddess Morrigan. Trying not to sound giddy and terrified I interrupted, my voice rasping out too harsh, too loud. "Thank you, sir. Shall we leave now?"

"Of course. If you will follow me." The deep timbre was replaced with a cold, professional sound.

I only hoped he would understand why I could not be more open. I thought I saw pain in his cobalt eyes. *Oh Gods!* Does he not realize this is killing me, too? To have him stand in front of me in the flesh and not touch him, show him how I feel. Knowing I had no choice but to heed my head, knowing an eternal love was growing deep within my chest. To know, even though I could feel his breath on my cheek, I could not lay the barest of caresses on his hand or show him the emotions trying to spill its way from my soul.

We followed Kyle in silence, through the clanging airport and to a sky-blue pickup. My favorite color. The height and ruggedness of the truck seemed out of proportion with my world and our need for secrecy.

After he placed our luggage securely in the uncovered cab, he opened the passenger side doors for us. Aine and Jack climbed into the back, while Kyle helped me to the front. His hand was tense and clasped almost painfully on my arm.

"Sorry if it's not fancy enough for you." There was an odd pause as we locked eyes. "My home is in the hills. Truck and horse are the only way." He smiled as his eyes burned with a craving to inflict as much hurt as he must have felt.

I controlled myself. Barely. *Why is he mad at me?* I would not have chosen to cause him any more pain then he already faces. *He is too bold.* I spun out of the truck and plopped into the back next to Jack, pulling him next to me. If Kyle wanted to be childish, I would be childish.

What was it a human would say? Their expressions were stellar. Jack grinned from ear to ear, the heat of his ego rising like molten rock from Fay Mountain. Kyle was cooler than ice, silent in fury. Aine looked confused and hurt. The long ride was uncomfortable. I am not sure who would have broken first. Thankfully, Kyle pulled to the side of the road.

"Are we walking from here?" Aine asked.

"No. The man, Fearghus, said you were looking for stone artifacts representing each of the Celtic Gods. Correct?"

"Yes. Lady Shayla will need to examine each carefully. That may take hours, or even days."

"There is a cavern not too far from here that's rumored to hide a stone carving of Cliodna, the Goddess of beauty and the nether world. It is said she is in the form of a sea bird. There are many caves or tombs such as this scattered throughout northern Scotland. Many originated in other parts, but when the English gained control, most were brought here to the Highlands for safekeeping. I thought since we were passing by, you might wish to stop."

Jack interrupted. "I think we should continue to your place instead and start fresh in the morning. We have traveled a long way, and...Lady Shayla is sure to be tired."

We needed more care. I did not need people referring to me as Princess. This trip was proving to be ill-ridden and ill-prepared for. Aine's shoulders were rigid.

"I think Mr....I don't believe we know your last name."

"Kyle is okay. Do you want to look now, or some other time? There are relics all around this area."

"We've decided on tomorrow." Jack insisted.

I pulled away from him. I may have encouraged his behavior, but it was time for a reminder of how I truly felt, and who I was.

"I think Kyle is correct. Unless you and Aine are too tired, I will look now."

"Go now," Aine said. "I would only ask, unless you need me to come along, that you let me wait here. I am tired and would like to rest."

"Jack will stay with you. This is Kyle's homeland, and he is the guide, after all. He will know where the statue is." I climbed out of the truck. Jack nearly tripped me, following on my heels. He leaned toward me, much too close.

"This is not a good idea, Shayla. We are here to keep you safe, not let you run off with a stranger."

"No, Jack," Aine said. "Lady Shayla is correct. Kyle knows the area and should be the one to go with her. Unless you think she should roam the Highlands alone?"

Jack sighed.

It was a good thing he recognized the only choice left him.

"It is settled. If you are ready, Kyle, I am too."

Kyle and I walked for thirty minutes before finally reaching the entrance of a cave. "Here. The statue is inside." Kyle took a seat on a fallen log.

"You are not coming with me?"

"No. I was told you were to study the relics either alone, or with your female companion." The left corner of his mouth curled up, smug as a lion with a full belly.

"Fine. Wait here. I should be able to find it easily enough."

"You'll find it, all right. It is about fifteen feet inside and to your left. No one said I couldn't tell you where they are in the caves. Hurry up, would you? I didn't get much sleep last night and want to get home to relax."

His arrogance caused my cheeks to redden, but I refused to be baited. I went inside. There was very little light, and I let my Fay sight guide me. Closing my eyes, a faint outline appeared behind my lids. There, just to the left as Kyle said. The statue glowed a brilliant blue green, a water God, no doubt, but not a God of death. I walked up to the statue and laid my hands on it, chanting.

"Guide me, my Goddess. Show me where I am to go to become what I am meant to be. I ask you, Goddess, show me the way."

I opened my eyes. The statue still glowed, but I felt no different. I had received a gift given to a faithful believer and thanked the Goddess, despite the meagerness.

"Guide and protect the land and people, Goddess."

I did not want any Deities showing their displeasure. I learned long ago to be thankful for every bequest. An ungrateful Fay could feel the consequences in surprising ways. With the glow of the relic behind me, I turned to the inside of the cavern. Moss outlined the moist walls with hints of stone striking through. The floor felt as soft. I expected to see the same on the floor. Instead, I found a trail of rich black dirt. I retraced my steps back out of the cave. Kyle stood at the entrance, waiting.

"I was beginning to wonder if you were going to come out, or whether I had to come in and find you."

"Why would you feel it necessary? The cave is not deep."

"Caves frighten girls."

"I am not a child, and I do not treat you as such. If you continue to start fights, then I will have no choice but to release you from this duty. Are you going to act like an adult or not?"

"Lady...Princess...Witch...whatever. I would love nothing more than to end this arrangement. But there is something you should know before I walk away from you and your friends."

"What might that be?"

My hands clenched at my hips. They were itching to slap him, but I did not dare. I remembered the personal tale of death he had confided to me. I did not want to rush it along, no matter how much he agitated me. I did not know whether I was physically stronger than a mortal, or if my powers unknown were lying in wait to defend me. Either way, I had been told to beware.

"Fearghus, your friend, boss, whichever, mentioned if you refused to work with me, he would need to know. It sounded ominous. Are you sure you want me to go?"

"I wish for it more than anything else, but as you have reminded me, I do not have a choice. And your attitude will not get in my way."

I knew what the message meant. If I did not follow the path laid before me, then upon my return, I would become Aidan's bride.

"Good." He turned and headed back to the truck. "Now if you don't mind, I am ready to leave. I want to be home before it gets too late."

He and I were going to have to work this out. The human world was going to be harder, and more painful, than I had ever imagined.

Chapter Eight

STAYING AT KYLE'S HOME

The ride was breathtaking. Kyle's home nested in a wonderland, surrounded by rugged peaks and forests.

Was it to keep the world out or to keep him in?

He had not misled us. It would be impossible to reach his home any other way. The house had been in his family for generations and though very old, was still habitable and practical. After a short tour, he assigned each of us rooms. His own room was a single, high loft, an aerie as far away from ours as possible. It gave me pause, even knowing he would not realize I was coming, and would assume his guests would want privacy. Aine's room and mine, rich with the smell of polish and clean linens, faced each other. Jack's room was further down the hall, pervaded with dust motes.

"I did not realize I would be innkeeper to three people.

When I was hired, it was for two, a single man and woman.

"When were you hired?" Aine asked.

"Two weeks ago. I needed the time to buy plane tickets and get the money from your solicitor."

"You were hired two weeks ago? And we were told yesterday." I knew it was a mistake thinking out loud, but I was confused and wanted answers.

"I imagine Fearghus hired him shortly after I told your father of my intent to wed you," Jack replied. "Fearghus was furious. He told your father, if you did not know whom you wanted by now, then you never would. Your mother suggested this trip, saying I should go with you. It would give us a chance to become closer."

Jack's expression was stoic as he looked from me, to Aine, and back. I trembled. I am careless. How many more levels of secrets are going to be revealed? Father claimed he had not told Mother of his intentions, yet she suggested the trip two weeks ago? Why would he not tell her, or why not tell me she mentioned it. And if not before, why not last night? Jack's mouth needed a good binding under the circumstances.

"Hey! I don't mean to interrupt, but I have some things I need to do. I'll meet you in the kitchen in two hours."

Kyle strode from the hall and headed toward the stairs leading to his room. I had not meant to be too eager, following the swagger of his torso with my eyes. The man now consumed my waking hours, as much as he lived in my dreams.

Coming to my senses, I saw Aine smiling and Jack fuming.

"Jack, I need to talk with you privately." I turned to walk the length of the living room and out the front door where I waited. Jack followed with Aine on his heels.

"Yes? Princess?" His sarcasm showed how much he disliked using my title.

Strange how love chooses to change people in the blink of the Goddess's eye....

"You have to be more careful of what you say and around whom."

"Yes, Jack." Aine agreed, as she paced the narrow deck. "If Kyle was anyone else, we could be in serious trouble."

Is Aine becoming increasingly moody?

"I will not allow you to jeopardize this. Either start acting as a Fay Guard or go home. You are taking everything personal, and I cannot allow it to continue. This whole journey is not about you or me. It is about the Fay." I took a deep breath. "And please believe me when I tell you, I do not care for you more than as a friend. You must stop acting jealous. I have not given my Father, or you, my answer. So, either way, I would tread carefully around me, if I were you."

"What do you mean you have not decided? Your only other choice is Aidan." Jack spat over the railing. "Would you choose him over me?"

"You presume you are the only choice for King. Maybe I like none, as much as I do you, but there are others. You are my friend. If I have to sacrifice love for duty, then I will. I would like to have a friend by my side. But know this... if you do become my groom, I will not submit to you. My line will continue to rule. I will be the ultimate ruler, Jack. I want you to think of what I have said and think hard. And I am not completely without intelligence, even though I feel without at the moment. I want you to make things right between you and Aine. I will need both of you." Not giving either of them a chance to reply, I ducked inside and headed to my room. Aine followed.

"I wish to speak with you, my Lady."

"Of course. What is the matter?"

"I wish to return home. I thought I could handle watching you with him, but I cannot. I love him too much. I would not cause you any problems, but please do not torture me. Allow me to go home." Tears fell freely down her reddened cheeks.

"If you wish to go home, I will not stop you, no matter how much I need you. I did not realize how much you have grown to care for Jack."

"I have loved him longer than I can remember. I hoped when you wed, he would forget his feelings for you, but there is no hope. He would now be King to your Queen." Aine sobbed.

"Ah, Aine, please do not cry. I know not what you must have heard and seen, but I promise I no more wish to wed Jack, than you want me to. I love another." Shocked, I paused and held my breath.

She hiccupped. "You truly mean this!"

"Yes," I whispered.

"The man in the water?"

"How do you know about him?"

"I saw shadows, but more, I sensed the two of you together. Is he the one you love?"

"Yes, he is the one, but I cannot have him."

"Oh, Princess. The Law. I am so sorry. Your love is even more hopeless than my own."

"It is not for you to worry about. Are you going to tell Jack how you feel? Or am I?"

"I cannot. I must wait for him to come to me."

"Since he will not be heading any farther my way, I think we will push him along to you. The next time he seeks you out, tell him. He needs to know someone loves him."

"But what are we to do about your problem? You must find your Power and a King."

Aine may not believe she and Jack had a chance, but at least she focused on my problem. Now, she would keep by my side, our problems entwined.

"I do not know. All I can be sure of, it will not be Aidan or Jack. My priority must be the Power, or else there will not be a choice of King." Then sighing, "Oh, Goddess, please grant me more strength, so that I may better serve you."

"Let me get this right," a voice drawled from the doorway. "If I help you find this power...whatever it is, you have to marry Jack...in there. If I don't help you, or if you fail, then you marry some guy named

81

Aidan. So...how do you get out of marrying either? How suitable for a Princess to have such a tempting choice."

Chapter Nine

THE BARRIER

I heard it loudly, his sarcastic curse. Of the three of us, I did not know who was shocked more.

"Well? Am I getting this straight or not?"

"How long have you been standing there? Never mind. You should not concern yourself with my problems. It is who I am, who my people are. I am sorry, but it is all I can say on the matter. You only need to know this and only this. Love has never, nor ever will, come into this decision."

I tried giving him enough information. To explain what being Fay meant, without telling him who my people are. But, how should I make him understand something I have never believed in myself?

"I don't get it. You are supposed to be a Princess, but can't choose who you marry? Am I missing something important, or are you and your people nuts?"

"I am so sorry, Princess. I should not have used your title. Now he knows."

"Do not be upset. He knew before we came here."

Aine frowned. "He is the man from the water. The dream come to life. A wish made by a dying mother granted..." Her eyes widened.

I did not know if I was the only one who felt the change of vision, and the grays turning bluer, but the world shifted and inhaled.

"A wish made and fulfilled, and nothing would stand in its way." I heard Aine's voice, a whistle in the wind.

Goddess grant us the knowledge we require... My life...Kyle's...all of our lives altered forever, the pieces in place. I realized my fate to love a dying man, to grant my mother's wish, and to know a love greater than my mother's own.

But what of theirs?

I was positive Kyle was to love someone he could never have. Or was the meaning higher, and to know something greater than his impending death? Aine's anxious chant may not have been cast the true way, but it still had effect. Life was fraught with beginnings and endings, and new life. Will Aine also finish something she or her family started?

My journey began to bring life back to my dying people, and for me to avoid a marriage. Now my destiny branched, a tree in the wind.

"I have done more than enough intruding for one night. I will leave you two alone to sort out this mess. I am sorry, Princess. I fear I have made your life more difficult."

Aine had over-stepped her bounds, and there was nothing either of us could do about it.

"What did she mean by all that? Who is a dream come to life and what is the wish granted?"

The torment was exquisite. Hope and suffering in the same gasp.

"You are the dream come true, and my mother's dying wish for me. Aine is right. My life will be harder than before. On my own, I might have stopped this, whatever is happening between us. Now it will be as if we are fighting the Deities themselves."

No matter the past, the Fay will never allow any of us to be with a human. Especially their Princess.

"Deities?" Kyle's breath caught in his throat, and a comical smile emerged. "Wait! You said the man of your dreams, and we are being literal here, right?"

The smile buoyed me. Seeing it was worth any pain I would go through. He knew what he meant to me. Part of him reveled in the knowledge, but the sensible part knew, no matter how much I desired him, we could never be.

"You are right. If I was ever able to be with the man I chose, it would be you. The heavens are surely envious of my love."

"Why can't we be together? I am telling you, Lady, I want you as much, maybe more."

He stepped nearer to me, clenching both fists, his fierce gaze set. He would never let me walk away. My body tingled with his close familiarity. He was willing to fight for me... for us. I trembled knowing if he continued, not only would I die, but he would also, curse or no curse.

"Kyle, you must understand. We can never go farther than what we have. I wish it were not so, but it is. Unless you accept this, then my friends and I will have to find a different guide, no matter what Fearghus has to say about it. My life and yours depend on it."

Not wanting to insist on our destination anymore, I stepped towards him and closed the door. I could hear Aine and Jack yelling at each other in the next room, but I did not have the energy to intervene. They could work out their own troubles. Mine were bigger than I wanted, or could handle. Flinging myself onto the bed I did not care enough to even remove my clothing. I only wanted to make the pain lancing through my body go away. Sleeping had seemed to be the only way to hide from it.

A hand caressed my shoulder, but I refused to acknowledge it. Like a balm, my dreams were peaceful and full of happy times from my past. I thought I heard a voice. "Fine. You won't come to me then I'm coming after you."

Warm water drifted against my body and I thought I breathed in the sweet scent of roses.

Blinking I opened my eyes. Kyle relaxed in the pool across from me, his body covered in bubbles. Roses could not smell as sweet or seductive, as the feast my eyes beheld.

Grinning, sexy, he raised one soapy hand at me. I could feel myself shaking my head no. Raising his left eyebrow, he opened and closed the hand, now only a scant few inches away from me. Looking at the hand, I could feel my body responding to the feel of his eyes roaming over me. I quivered. *Why has no other man affected me this way?*

"Why won't you come and join me? We both know you want too."

My knees buckled. I needed to get away from him, but I could not figure out how. I, a member of the Fay, a Princess, full of magic and immortality, could not escape one mortal man's dream. Even though the dream had begun as mine, it was now his. The details were intricate and stunning.

"Where is this?" I blurted out. "I had not realized the flowers here were so beautiful."

That was smooth. I am worse than Jack. I no longer control my own thoughts or my mouth as well.

"None can compare to your beauty. Your hair is the color of the blackest rose I have ever seen, your skin smooth as satin and white as fresh snow. My God, woman, your breasts would make a sane man foolish with the need to touch their curves. Even the small scar right above your eye shows determination to survive. Your height teases all of me, knowing you are a woman who can stand on her own, and will never let a man own her." His voice grew husky. "I crave your legs holding me against you."

I do not remember the span of time, or whether it had been his growl of hunger or my own, but I fell into his embrace, not caring about tomorrow. The heat in his kiss turned the forest around us into an inferno.

For a moment, the intensity of what was happening drowned out who we were and created a sea of desire. Nothing could force me to stop. Kyle was the very breath my body craved in the deep ocean. Without him at this moment in time, I could not have gone on. Reason crept on me as our clothes faded away. I gasped against his cheek.

"Kyle, I want this more than anything, but we have to stop. What we do in our dreams, affects our lives."

"I don't care. To love you, be with you, is more important now than what comes. Don't you understand? My death... let me die knowing your love."

He grasped for me as I slipped away as far as I could. I tried to climb out of the water, but a barrier stopped me. It may be his dream, but I never lost myself so completely I could not regain control.

"What if you're not meant to have control?" He looked hungry and feral.

My belly started to knot. "How? How did you know what I was thinking?" *How could he have known?*

"How else? I can feel what you're feeling. Know what you're thinking. Why? Don't you know what's going on in my mind?"

He was teasing me, testing me, wanting me to take the bait and connect with him, but I could not. His desires would pour into me, and I would be lost. It was no dream. It was a fantasy taking control of each part of me.

Who was more worth saying no to, her people or him? "Yes... no, I cannot. Too many depend on me. There are too many lives at stake for me to give in to you. I am sorry."

91

I turned from him and focused all my inner weight to escape. I had to get away from him, from here. But, no matter how hard I tried, the barrier would not break. Something stronger than I was pressing back, holding us there. My breath came in short bursts.

Another Fay knew what we were doing and kept me inside.

I pulled again, this time, against myself.

"Hey! Calm down. You're freezing me."

That did it. The shock of the icy water and his words broke the spell. I pressed one final time, and with a thud, fell through to the floor alongside my bed.

"Tonight, can never happen again. Let me out of your fantasy. Now!"

Kyle peeked over the side. "Look...I am not controlling any of this, you are. If you really wanted the dream to stop, then it would. I just sat in the water wishing you join me." He pouted.

Goddess!

He hurt. I could not stand to let the pain in, and there was nothing I could say to end it. Maybe It was better this way. He could go on with his life as though we had never met.

"No, you don't. I am glad I met you and this happened, even if you are not...even though I am the man of your dreams."

I heaved myself up. "That is just it. You are the man I have always wanted and needed. As I have said over and over, we are from two other worlds. There is nothing that will change that. If I could, I would. If I could leave here, I would. Do you not understand how much this is hurting me? What am I supposed to do? Walk naked through your home to the room you are allowing me to use, look down at myself and say...Wake! Up!"

I had noted I was back in his room, and the hysteria in my voice was telling. It was very unprincess-like. I did not care.

"Shayla, I'm not sure how to say this, but I am not asleep. You know, I have never been asleep when we are together."

Oh. Well. How was that possible?

I completely lost it. If there is one thing, I can be sure of, it's the fact of my body being in my bed and not here.

"If you are awake, then how? Only one of my people is capable of walking in someone else's dreams."

"You would not come to me, so I came to you. We are in what I call dream waking. I have always been able to travel this way. You are the first one who has been able to interact with me as though we were both awake."

"Where are your families from?" I blurted.

"My fathers' family is from this land. We have been a part of Inverness as far as can be traced back. My mother's side came from an island in the Irish Sea. I don't know much about them, but it was said, the

94

women die shortly after the birth of their first male child."

"Where in the Irish Sea?"

"I don't know. No one does. The island was there one year and gone the next. Whoever tried charting its location got lost somehow. I doubt it vanished into thin air. Why? What does this have to do with us?"

It was near legendary in some circles. How many times had I heard of Fay men mating with mortal women? Why not Fay women mating with mortal men? Here was proof that it happened. At least he did not realize who the Fay were, but that did not help. How did I ask anything without telling?

"I guess it does not pertain to us. Now, how do we stop this dream waking of yours?"

"You are avoiding me." He grinned and glanced down at my nakedness. I felt like a spindly-legged newborn doe. "By finishing. Once it is begun, that is the only way out."

"By finishing..."

95

"...With you in the water here with me and continuing what we started. You see? This is no ordinary dream waking, but pure fantasy and ecstasy."

In one movement, he grabbed me around the waist and pulled me into the water, slamming me into his hard, slick chest. His heart pounded in tune with my own. His chest hair teased my aching breasts, as the water rolled frenzied around us.

"Please, Shayla. Finish this fantasy with me. Please say you will be mine, if only for tonight."

I answered with a kiss and a caress. With my hands exploring any part of him I could reach. My legs wrapped like ivy around his waist, and my hips worked their way down his body. He nearly slipped when my moistness touched and penetrated around his head.

"Yes! Yes!" His voice vibrated into each pore of my skin, releasing bursts of pleasure, leaving me quivering and shaking. He groaned, grabbing my thighs so fiercely, I might be bruised. My body acquiesced in anticipation of his movement. It was rapture.

Our lovemaking was fierce, knowing we could never be like this again. I froze, the thought of this moment ending, terrifying me. He did not move but gazed into my eyes. I saw the question deep within. I did not want to answer.

Instead, I pressed my face into his neck breathing in his skin's musk and oils. The scent was incredible, a heady spice I could not name. Something I had never smelled before. It served to heighten my need for him, for with him was the only way I would ever smell it again. Tears were smudging my cheeks.

"Please. Love me and hold me. Make me believe we can be together forever."

He kissed my tears, my eyelids and lips, covering each part of my face with his tenderness. "I will love you for all time."

Pushing me gently up, I wrapped my arms around his shoulders. Our lovemaking had started fierce. Now, the softness spared my heart. The deep fire now reached a radiant plateau, our climax beating as one.

We drifted.

I awoke, crying in my bed, clothes gone and an aching low in my stomach. It was the same sweet ache given to me when Kyle and I had made love in the Falls of Fay.

Was there truly more to this, than dreams and fantasies? What would become of us, once I returned home? Would I hold these exquisite moments with Kyle against the faithful husband I must eventually choose? Why have the Gods sent him to me now?

Chapter Ten

KYLE'S EX & A MOTHER'S LOSS

Instead of planning numerous day trips, Kyle packed enough supplies for several weeks on the road. We spent two days searching Northwest Scotland before arriving at Isle of Lochalsh, leading to the Isle of Skye. Kyle knew where most of the artifacts were, and we let him choose our stops. The nights were spent in quaint little houses turned into inns.

"We are being led in a circle," Jack complained.

"Grow up and shut up." Aine responded.

Our current hotel was run by a friend of Kyle's. I soon found out, this willowy stranger was his ex-fiancée, and her husband, his best friend.

Sophie defined gorgeous, with long lengths of red hair and the softest blue eyes I have ever seen. Comfortable and nonchalant, Kyle introduced us as archeologists searching for lost relics of the Gods. Later, in our rooms, I fumed.

"Why did you nearly tell her the whole truth?"

"Sophie knows the location of three statues. She will show you."

"Yeah...right..."

Kyle's laughter barked like a dog. "You're jealous. I can't believe it. She's married, for crying out loud."

"I am not jealous, and even if I were, what does it matter? So there really is nothing to be jealous about." As I stomped to the lobby, I knew what a windstorm felt like. The beautiful rooms around me did not lighten my mood, even with their scattered paintings of our enchanted island and how man thought Fay looked.

The ears are wrong...

Home. It called me. Each moment harder than the last. Each minute pulling at me. Being with Kyle was magical and gratifying, our days spent looking for artifacts, and the nights, a sweet torment. We lived for the temptation of fulfilling our fantasies, but the pull of home never left me.

Lying in bed that evening, I wondered how Father fared.

Was he being forced to consummate his marriage, or did the Elders get what they wanted and now left him alone?

I awoke standing in the throne room, my Father in front of me weeping. An ethereal breeze lifted strands of my hair as I looked around the expansive room. No one else was there. Slipping silently to his side, I laid my hand on his quaking shoulder. "Father, why do you cry so?"

He shuddered and gaped at me, surprise and fear on his loving face. It nearly broke my heart.

"I do not understand. How are you here before me, when I know you are gone for all time?"

"Gone..."

"I received word today of your death in the human world."

Gone?

His words echoed inside me like a yawning cavern, the torment and pain making me doubt my existence.

"I do not understand. Who would tell such lies to you?"

"Lies? I pray for lies. Even now, Jack and Aine travel by sea, bringing your body home. At first, I thought they were mistaken, for you did not fade. Then, I was reminded of the Fay who had fallen before you in the human world. They had not faded until they were brought home. The same is for you."

Father had never been a fanciful or delusional man. He must believe in my death, yet I knew I dreamed.

"On what day did I die?"

He sobbed. "Your birthday."

"But, how is it you are weeping for me?"

I got no response. Not being able to reach him to reason, I attempted to reason with myself. My birthday fell a week from now.

"He has been here for the last three days. I am the only one allowed to enter." Fearghus stood behind me.

"You do not seem surprised at my appearance. Why is that?"

"You are not the first to die in no-Fay's-land. You shall know unrest until your body is returned."

"Die! I am not dead. Father said I died on my birthday. My birthday is not for another seven days. There is no limbo here, only a dream."

"So...dream waking is your true power. Why do you not return home if your quest is finished? Before you truly die and all hope is lost?"

"Because dream waking is not my true power. I was able to do it before I left home."

It was all the detail Fearghus needed to know, but his voice still grew feral as he stepped near to my ear. "Then you must hurry and find your true power. This is more than just walking in dreams; it is a glimpse into your future. A sign from the Gods of what is to come. I wish for you to learn your heritage while you are gone, not die from it. I give you five days. If you have not evolved by then, you should return no matter what."

For the first time that I knew of, fear edged his will. "You know I cannot. I will not return to be given to Aidan, nor will I stand by while his family lays claim to what is rightfully mine."

"I never wished Aidan on you, only for you to take your place as all Fay must do. As your Father did before you, and his Father before him. Rule us, Princess. Rule all the Fay."

He came around to me. The determination in his eyes shook mountains.

Drama for my benefit or his?

"You speak as though more than my taking the throne is at stake."

"It is. My future is also at stake. I am fading but cannot or will not rest until you sit safely on the throne with your chosen King."

I had an answer for him. I needed to believe Fearghus was concerned more for our people than I had given him credit for. "I give you my word as Princess of Fay, I will return in five days' time, with or without my power. You must also give your word to help me out of a wedding to Aidan."

His forehead furrowed and his eyes pierced into mine, but he finally nodded. "On your arrival, if Aidan is not for you, then another suitable husband shall be chosen."

"I wish I could believe that, but you know as I do, the other Elders must also say so. You will need to convince them. Will you? Can you?"

"Do not worry yourself overly much. They will follow my lead when the time is right. I suggest you call on as many of the male Fays you can between now and then. By peering into their dreams, you will know who to choose."

He did not bring up Jack, and I did not ask.

"It looks as though I now have more than one quest to accomplish in the human world. I must find the elusive true power and invade my fellow Fay's dreams."

How was that done anyway? I only dream
walked on a whim.

"I am not too old to know adolescent sarcasm
when I hear it. You need to hurry. Wake yourself and
start your new day."

He waved me away.

I woke with a start. *How did he do that?*

How was he able to cast me out of my own
dream? I flung off the thick blanket and made my way
to the bathroom. The morning sun burnished the
wood floor.

After a quick shower and dressing, I hurried to
the dining room. It was most likely too early to be
served. Grumbling, I did not know what it was that
harried me. The hotel stirred up an anxiety that
gnawed in me. Nearly reaching the dining room
doors, I changed my mind and veered to the front
doors and out. Out here was the sea and something to
eat. The water slapped against the piers, crispy and
refreshing. I wanted more than anything to dive in,
but people would find it strange to see a woman

swimming in the cold waters, especially on a brisk, December morning.

My birthday.

It stunned me when I thought about it. Six days from now, the 25th of December fell. Yule is said to be one of the few times during the year a Fay's powers are at their strongest. Those days are long gone. My birthday falling on Yule, was an interesting footnote, more than anything else.

Instead of a swim, I found a quiet tavern opening its doors to the sun.

"Hello, Miss. Can I get ye something?" The dear, old woman must have been near her 70th year.

"Aye, a cup of coffee would brighten my day and warm my sad soul." I tried using an accent. Kyle pointed out, even with the trace of Irish in my voice, I still sounded English.

"Good try Lass, very good try." The woman smiled, before showing me a seat and walking to the kitchen.

"Shayla? Shayla, where are you?"

I nearly jumped out of my seat. Looking around, I realized the only one to hear Kyle was me. He was pulling up a seat, inside my head.

Great. Just great.

"Shayla…"

NO!

Here I am sitting in a public place and he wants to dream play. Well, who is the authentic Fay here anyway? I turned my attention back to the room in front of me.

Pictures in varied frames covered most of the wall space. The subjects were diverse, from drawings of people, to photos of Scotland itself. Only one Fay picture was on the wall. It captured the moment a baby Fay got its wings. I was amazed how well humans could draw us, but not our homeland.

"I see ye noticed baby Fay. She was a wee bonny lass. I imagine she is long dead by now."

"You speak as though you know the Fay. Do not tell me you believe in such beings. In these times?"

"Of course, I do, and no, I fear I didna know her personally. It is said she was the kindest and fairest of all Fay. Do ye wish to know her name?"

Her eyes sparkled. Amusing both of us, she had lured me in, hook, line and sinker. "If you know her true name, then please whisper it to me."

The old woman bent down. Her breath reminded me of fresh sugar cookies and the honeyed smell of the Hill's wildflowers on my island. "Gwendolyn, Queen of the Fay."

She left coffee and cookies behind. I finally closed my mouth when she turned around and touched her finger to her nose. It seemed Fay had not entirely been forgotten. The proof of it lived in this quaint little place.

I turned my head and wiped the tears from my eyes. My mother, not personally known to these people, still impacted their lives somehow. Maybe it was their dreams. Gone from this earth, but never forgotten. Maybe it was what I needed to remember, to think of. Even though she had faded, she would forever be in our hearts and souls.

"Oh, Mother. Please forgive my anger at your leaving. I am so sorry; I just need you so!"

When I was able to open my eyes again, I saw Kyle standing in front of the tavern, looking through the window at me. His smile was distorted through the imperfect glass, but I recognized the amusement. I needed to shake off the confusion and turned as he ducked through the door. His height still caught me off guard.

"Thought you could get rid of me, huh? You forget. I know this town and the people in it. I saw Margaret through your eyes and knew where to come."

I decided to ignore yet another side to his alarming abilities. "Where are Jack and Aine? We need to continue looking for relics. I only have five days left in which to find the one, and then I must return home."

"Five! Why only five? Never mind... if five days is all I have left, then I need to start trying harder."

"Harder? What are you going on about now?"

"Why...winning your love."

"I am afraid I do not have time for such foolishness. Now, where is the next idol?"

"Someone's not a morning person. I was going to tell everyone over breakfast, but since you are in such a hurry, the first one is in Blaven, just at the foothills, with Portree Bay after. The next at Edinbane Cave on the coast Loch Snizort. The last is at Dunvegan Head."

I did not know where or what it was, but my ears shifted when Kyle said Dunvegan. I reached for reason, and knew it was not because Fay Island would be near. My homeland was not coming any closer than the Isle of Lewis, north of Stornoway.

What was it about the name that meant something to me?

"It is where you find your true power Princess" Fearghus boomed in my head.

"Is something wrong?"

"No. How many days do you think it will take us to get there?"

I still did not trust Fearghus, but I wanted to stop our journey as soon as possible. The statue could be anywhere, but I could not afford to be hasty.

My head should be swollen to the size of the moon with the company there.

"We can be in Blaven this afternoon, and then Portree by tonight, but we need to check in at the local inn beforehand. The next morning, we can head to Edinbane Cavern, then to Dunvegan and into the Hidden Lakes of Corra. There is supposed to be a tiny island in the center, named Corra's keep."

"We will be in Dunvegan in two days?"

"Yeah, if we push it. I was hoping to show you some of the sites here first."

"I am afraid I don't have the time this trip. I must be back at Cambletown Port in four days hence, ready to return home. If you could get me there in three, it would be better. We will make it there in time?"

"Sooner, if you want. It's fine by me. You're the boss. I guess we better round up your friends."

His pain was my own, and there was nothing I could do. I must hurry home before my disastrous fate came to pass. Now, it was my person at stake, as well as the other Fay. I was not a selfish person, but my death served to spur me on. Our fates all swung in the balance, like a noose in a sea squall.

Chapter Eleven
THE GODDESS OF DEATH

Except for an early lunch, the trip to Blaven was uneventful. I was not the only one to miss breakfast. Kyle suggested one of the local taverns, but we were rushed for time and grabbed sandwiches to go. Arriving at the cave in early afternoon, everyone stepped out of the truck without saying a word.

"I suppose we are expected to sit in the truck again," Jack commented, after holding out a hand to Aine in the back seat and making sure she was safely out.

"There is no reason for you to join us," Kyle replied, then paused in his steps to the forest. "Unless, of course, you want to join us. Or in any case, you can sit wherever you want."

Aine had admitted she and Jack were speaking more of themselves and to each other as familiar companions. This time to her seemed crucial. She was anxious and fretful.

"I think it is more prudent for Aine and me to stay behind. I just wanted us to have the choice, and I don't relish worrying about Shayla. Go and hurry it up."

Aine's sigh exploded like the Goddess's breath.

Kyle shrugged and led me into the trees and rocks. I waited for the usual tale of the area's history, his ritual enlightenment on our treks, but he merely strode along in front of me. We walked a long way into the woods in growing silence. Even the life of the forest would not respond to our steps. The world seemed a dull echo.

"Please, Kyle. I need a break. I did not sleep well last night." I sat on a comfortable looking outcrop.

His fierce anger struck me. "Whose fault is that? Because it sure is not mine..." He turned viciously and grabbed my arms, jerking me to my feet. "Who was it, Shayla? Who else did you lure to your bed?"

"I do not know what you mean."

He assumed. Since I refused to dream walk to him this morning, and he could not reach me last night, then I must have been with another.

"It is not what you think. I thought to explain. Now you act like a ninny."

His face reddened. "Fine! Explain! We don't have much farther to go, and a moment after that, we have to leave."

"I wish it were just that easy, but I am afraid it is not. We should reach the cave and talk of this later at the inn. Just trust me when I say there has been no other."

"Whatever. I never thought it. Let's just go."

I am not sure at what point I had decided, but I realized I had planned on telling him everything. Now, I was no longer sure. If he were so imprudent over missing one night with me, then he would be furious when he realized in a few days' time, we would never be.

The cave was like the others, as all caves tended to be, I suppose. Vines of ivy draped the entrance and made a fragrant curtain to guard the treasures inside. On the inside, soft ground and moss grew along the walls, fed by the moisture that ran down in tiny rivulets when the Goddess decided the earth needed fed. Though chill and winter was all around, the cave held spring firmly in its grasp.

As I made my way toward the back with my lamp, I sensed the death Fearghus had predicted. I did not want to call on unnecessary magic, lighting my way and giving the God or Goddess a reason for a tribute. Some Deities were arrogant. If you showed any amount of power, they assumed it their magic. And no matter which part of nature a Deity possessed, they all cycled life and death, a natural part of existence. A Fay needed to be cautious when approaching strange Gods and Goddesses. You never knew when Death itself would appear. I did not want to owe any part of Death.

I was too young to dwell on death and had been shocked to learn it would be so soon. If I could not stop it, then I needed to impress the Elders and name a successor. If I did not, Aunt Brigit and Aidan might convince them otherwise, and that would mean the end of our true way.

I lifted the light and let its soft radiance flow across the pale statue. My senses had served me well, for facing me stood the Goddess Aife. I took two deep breaths and placed my hands on her, chanting my request. I did not expect an answer. I was not sure I wanted one.

"Sweet child of Fay, Princess Shayla. I cannot wait to hold your young body in my arms. I shall open my heart in welcome to you. I do not have the relic you wish and can only promise your death will be sweet upon my lips."

She stirred, her eyes iridescent black lights. I was not sure I could move to speak. It was not often one prayed to the Goddess of Death. Some might believe she was cruel, but I knew better. She was simply telling me, as kindly as possible, nothing would stop my impending doom.

"Thank you, kind Goddess. Is there a penance you would require of me for this gift of your presence?"

Leaving an opening for a Goddess was risky, but Aife was known for justice.

"Nay, my child. There is nothing I wish from you now. I will take my boon in six days." The hem of her flowing black robe brushed my leg as she vanished.

I turned and left with a resigned sigh. Kyle stood at the entrance waiting. He had not offered to come inside with me, and though I knew it was for the best, it still bothered me.

Despite our nights of ecstasy, he grew more moody and bitter. This morning he teased me. Now, I was ignored like an ant at his feet. I could not fault him. He told me many times he loved me, but would never beg.

Maybe too many times.

The Gods chose to curse him as they did me, but he was oblivious of their manipulations, and of the concepts of fate and destiny. The Gods gave him his heart's desire, only to take it away from him.

"I am ready if you are."

"Whatever. Let's just get back."

"Wait... Kyle...tell me what is wrong."

He turned toward me so fast, I nearly ran into him. "Are you sure you want to know?"

"Of course, I do."

"You refuse to fight for us. You just give up. The woman of my dreams is not as strong as I once thought."

I did not expect the comment and froze, staring at his retreating back. A loss I did not want to accept welled up.

"I cannot allow myself to care for you," I shouted. "I must return home and you will not go with me. My people would kill you for even thinking of touching me."

Kyle disappeared.

I wiped the tears from my eyes and followed him back to the others. Aine's senses were keen. She knew before we emerged from the woods, her eyes picking out my discolored face and eyes. I knew she wanted to talk, but I shook my head before climbing in the back seat. Looking out the window at the surrounding forest, I contemplated my future.

If I survived beyond my birthday, would I ever know true happiness? Could I choose a King who would never know my love? I would be forced to have a child with him to prolong my family line. I know my responsibilities to my people, but my heart was screaming out for Kyle's love. I should be dream walking, choosing my husband at these idle times.

Feeling the seat next to me give way, I turned to see Aine sitting beside me. We were moving again.

"When did we take off?"

"A few minutes ago."

She moved closer to me and nodded her head. I bent into her so she could whisper. I didn't know why she did it, but I needed her companionship. Placing my forehead to hers I smiled as she smiled softly in return.

"We are on our way to Portree. Kyle said it should only take a couple of hours to get there."

"After we leave the cave at Portree," Kyle added, "it will take thirty minutes to get to the Inn between there and Edinbane Cave. I suggest everyone get an early night so we can get an early start in the morning. I am expected back at Sophie's place for Yule."

"Of course," Aine responded. "Shayla, will we make it home in time for our own Yule celebration?"

I opened my mouth to reply, but Kyle interrupted.

"What! You mean you haven't received orders yet? You will be home in time, according to Miss Princess. You only have a few days left here."

Aine's looked at me, confused, and I looked at her and shook my head letting her know I did not wish to speak of it. She turned her head and stared out the window, as Jack also stared out in the distance.

Now they are all upset with me. What else will go wrong on this perfectly hopeless and lousy day?

The decision to agonize over events only made the future worse, so I leaned my head against the soft seat of the truck and tried to sleep. I found myself pulled back home and standing in the garden looking into the falls.

In someone else's dream.

"I wish you to be here. Do not fret, Princess, your companions believe you are asleep. As you have no doubt figured out, I can read your thoughts, so there is no reason for you to speak out loud." Fearghus stood softly beside me. "I choose the Garden because your father has decreed it off limits."

I wanted to ask a lot of whys.

"Your future has not changed. You shall still die on your birthday in a plane crash. I am warning you in advance."

I had just thought of flying home that morning to save time.

"I fear there is more," he continued. "You realize by now, I am able to dream walk."

"Yes." I spoke out loud. Fearghus in my mind unnerved me. "But why have you not told anyone of this? It is truly a wonderful gift and would be cherished by everyone. To think that an Elder still held such magic..."

"You do not have the experience, or you would realize, if some Fay knew, they would loathe me, even attempt to exile me. Their own fear would overrule any admirable thoughts they might have."

"Fear? We are not allowed to show true feelings."

"Just because it is against the Law to act emotional and unreasonable does not stop it, does it?

Some would contrive me a disturbance and rule breaker if they knew of my abilities."

"You are too honorable of a man to show your emotion. We may have disagreed many times in the past, but I know this to be true of you."

"I fear I cannot agree. Many times, I have looked into other's dreams. Even though it was for the good of the Fay, it was still wrong. It is how I now know the intentions of Brigit if you should fail."

His statement washed away any thoughts on the ethics of invading another's dreams. The mention of Aunt Brigit made my hackles rise. I turned and spat my question at Fearghus.

"And just what are her intentions?"

"The death of your Father and her rule over the Fay. When we were warned of your death, your Father showed his pain openly. He upholds the law any other time, but when it comes to you, he holds nothing else sacred. Brigit will use his display of emotions against him. She will point how weak he is and how he is no longer fit to rule. In private, she will whisper thoughts

126

of suicide to him. I fear, if he does not take his life, it will not matter. She will devise a way to kill him herself."

"How is that possible? He may not have any of the great powers, but he is still King of Fay. Our people may be angry at his emotional display, but they will not stand aside and watch him be killed. Everyone would fear the wrath of the Gods falling upon them. It is as if Brigit pretends to be Goddess herself."

"She is clever. If he dies the way she wishes, none will know he was murdered. I cannot say anything openly to stop it, or I will admit to dream walking. I am suspect in certain circles already. And there is not enough time for a Trial by Magic."

"Then I will not travel by plane. It is simple as that."

It was not that simple. I was going to die, and there was nothing either of us could do about it. The Fates had already decided on my fortune, and I had to accept it.

"Princess, as always I will attempt plans to help you. Now, I must prepare for my trying day, and you have a cave to explore."

He was gone and I opened my eyes to a beautiful lake in front of me.

Chapter Twelve

DEATH REVEALED YET
AGAIN

Kyle led me down the side of the cliffs, but where the cavern entrance should have been, a pile of rocks lay.

"Unless you can move those boulders, Miss Princess, we are not getting inside."

I ignored him and turned to slowly make my way back up the side. The freshly fallen snow made the trip down dangerous, and the climb up promised to be just as challenging. I proved I needed no help from Kyle.

Back at the truck and on our way, Aine urged me to cover up and try to sleep. No one asked what had happened, since I failed once again in finding my power.

What was the point?

We arrived at Edinbane Inn just as dusk fell and retired early for a fresh start in the morning. I slept fitfully, not wanting to meet Death in my dreams. The others refused to share their own thoughts, and I felt more and more isolated. Still tormented by dream remnants of Kyle and I, we drove to the next cave. Aine grabbed another on-the-go breakfast, and though the food smelled delicious, I could not force myself to eat more than a bite or two.

More snow had fallen during the night, and it took us longer than planned to reach our destination, the sun had just past midday.

Kyle climbed out of the truck and grabbed gear from the back. His hasty retreat made it hard to understand his words.

"Let's go. We have to walk about thirty minutes, before reaching the incline into the cave."

On a whim, I turned toward Aine and Jack. "Please come along with us this time. I realize the moments you spend alone mean a lot to the both of you, but I think you should be there." Asking them to give up their time alone was hard, but something inside of me had pushed.

"Of course, Shayla. Is something wrong?" Aine asked.

"Yes, Princess. What can we do to help?"

I might have corrected Jack for using my title, but who cares anyway? I did not care on reason of Death. A part of me analyzed the melancholy that crept up on me. My impending death was openly affecting the way I behaved. Being Fay, it was not allowed.

But being Princess and Fay is not going to stop my death either.

"Shayla?" Aine reached out and touched my arm.

"I am fine. Just be there, is all."

I waited for the both of them to nod and climbed out of the truck, barely noticing the dense forest on one side of us and the docile water on the other. Seeing the thin parting Kyle had disappeared into, I started down the path to my destiny. The trail was barely passable. It was apt.

When we caught up with Kyle, he was staring at a hole in the ground. Aine and Jack stepped up on either side of me, neither saying a word. I guess they realized talking to me had not done any good.

"This is where we go in. Aine, you and Jack stay here to keep the ropes secure. I'll go down first and hold them at the bottom for the Princess." He grimaced and straightened his back. "It's about a twenty-foot drop, so be careful. You can climb, right?"

Kyle dropped a light down the dark hole, before lowering himself inside. I thought of myself as bold, not frightened of small or dark areas, but that yawning gap snaked through my miserable irritation to terrorize me. My only saving grace was the knowledge I had no choice any more in what I did. It was that, and Kyle standing on the bottom. He gave me the strength and fury to carry on.

I grasped the rope with both hands and felt for the earth's nether way with my feet as Kyle had done.

About a foot down, the hole widened to reveal a glittering cavern, its walls encrusted with precious gems. The mortal's world placed value on certain minerals and rocks, and I was surprised they had not destroyed the cavern with their greed of money. Magic protected these types of places.

I thought of Kyle and realized greed did not seem to be in his blood. He was a rarity among both human and Fay. My loss of him added to the brightness of my own death. At least then, I would not miss him anymore.

The grip of his strong hands around my waist brought me back to the present and what I had to do. I allowed the sigh building up release. It shuddered past my lips and for one brief moment, I lost myself in his touch.

"Are you alright? I know the climb is nerve wrecking, but you did great." Kyle's voice soothed, touching even deeper inside me.

The cave and the closeness changed his manner. I wondered if the constant closeness was bothering him too, but I knew the answer to that.

I cleared my throat. "I'm fine...I just...what I mean is...oh, can we just hurry please?" I'm stuttering, I can't believe it. I've never stuttered before.

"Sure. You just looked spooked for a moment there. The statue is back this way. It is said to be at the end of this stream."

Looking down, I noticed the stream was a dry impression in the floor. If there had ever been water flowing here, it had been hundreds of years ago. Kyle pulled away.

"The statue is just beyond this turn. Do you want me to wait here for you, or go along and light the way?"

His voice was no longer smooth and caressing, but coolly professional. He would do whatever I commanded. I was his boss. Not wishing for the hurt I felt to be heard, I controlled my voice and commanded him as though he were my subject at court.

"You can wait here; I will not need the light. I do not need you."

I had wanted no misunderstandings. I did not want him to follow me. Not only might he be hurt for what he might see or hear, but I also feared for his life. Of course, my voice gave me away, becoming deeper at the end of my Princess act.

Not wanting to hear or sense his pity, I turned and escaped down the tunnel wiping tears along the way. I struck a small amount of light magic and the walls spiraled to life. I should have stayed and faced Kyle. What I found waiting for me was worse than any pain he might have caused.

Gwyn Ap Nuad. The first King of Fay, and lord of the underworld, stood in front of me in all his cold, burning glory.

He towered at least two feet above my head. It is said the statues were erected to be larger than life, but I would believe this one was shorter than true size.

He had been handsome, his features enhanced by the white stone he was carved of, and the shadows playing against the magic of the cave. Even the smile on his face was smug and eloquent, as if he had just pleasured a ladylove. I wondered whether a woman had been responsible for carving his facial features. Surely, no man would make his lips as full, or his eyes seem so moist and round. His eyebrows even cocked up just so, making him seem a mighty eagle in flight.

Lost in admiration, his smile grew deep and irresistible.

Was it for me? How? Stone cannot move, and there was not enough magic left in the human world to cause such. Was it a spell?

I felt my hand reaching up to caress his face and that lovely smile. I could feel the cool stone beginning to press against my breast.

"No! Princess, do not touch him. I feared this when I heard the human say you were coming here. He is responding to your magic. If you touch him, he may capture you."

So?

There was panic in Fearghus' voice, but so much of me wanted the scintillating tranquility Gwyn Ap Nuad offered.

"You know I have to. It is the only way to be sure he does not hold my true gift. I have no choice. Help me to touch him without me wanting all that he has to offer and letting him capture me. How do I accomplish this without this fear building inside me? You know as I do, the gift will not come if there is terror in my heart."

"You must offer him something more valuable than yourself."

"More valuable?" The King's voice sung like sweet nectar, beckoning me to come into his embrace. "What could be more valuable than the future Queen of Fay? Luscious and alive, what could compare? Her beauty I could pluck. It is worth more power and wealth than either of you could ever hope to possess. What shall you offer for her young supple body?"

"You are correct. I have nothing else to offer. I know my fate and I am to die soon enough. May I wait until then to offer myself to you?"

"Why should I wait for a dead Queen, when I can embrace the living one as she stands before me now?"

As she stands now? He gave me the answer.

"You! Shall wait. For I am the Queen of Fay, no longer Princess and you, Gwyn Ap Nuad, are not my King."

I stood straight. He was my subject and not the King of My Death.

"Very good. Very good indeed."

I thought it was a compliment.

"Queen of Fay, lay your sweet hands upon my own and see if you find powers from me. If you fail, then I will claim you upon your deathbed, and make you mine. Before your sweet body begins to fade, of course."

Now I have two deities waiting for payment upon my death. I reached my hand out to him,

138

caressing his hands, thinking to assuage him. The statue felt like a retiring room's warming stone, the power underneath pulsating just out of reach. With my mind, I pulled at the trophy, my efforts increasing against the sheer muscle of it. I tried coaxing it, kissing it with words and lips. Frustrated, I gave it one pull of absolute force. There was laughter. Annoyed, I stepped back.

"I shall enjoy spending an eternity with you."

"I hope the fates are wrong and I die an OLD... HAG..."

Gwyn Ap Nuad vanished, his laughter echoing against the shimmering walls.

"My Queen, I fear your fading will be too soon, no matter how old you may, or may not be."

"Queen? I am not your Queen yet. It was a game. I have yet to return home alive and get crowned."

"In some eyes you may not be Queen, but I saw what happened here. I say you are the Queen of Fay."

And with that, Fearghus vanished as well.

"Wonderful! Will no one stay around long enough to help me?"

"Did you say something?" I turned and saw Kyle coming up behind me. There were tears in his eyes, and I wondered how much he had heard.

"It is not important. Can we get out of here, please?"

He nodded, before taking my hand in his, leading the way back. Halfway up the rope, I began to shake and he helped me to climb the rest of the way. Once on top, refusing to hand me over to Jack, he carried me back to his truck.

Chapter Thirteen

THE FADING HAD BEGUN

"Shayla, are you all right?" Aine's voice wafted in the haze over me.

I opened my eyes and found my head in her lap. She must have understood the confusion I was feeling.

"You passed out. Kyle had me climb into the back seat so he could lay your head in my lap. I ask again, are you all right?"

"I am fine. Just very tired is all."

She frowned, not believing a word I had said. "Perhaps you should see your reflection, before making such statements."

She took a mirror from her purse and handed it to me. I had not realized, until then, how diligently I avoided my own reflection. Inside, I saw a desperate and dying woman looking at me. My eyes were puffy, and my nose red from crying. There were dark circles under my eyes, and their color duller than stone. My face no longer held a soft, happy look.

But the thing that frightened me the most was the translucent pitch of my skin. As I stared, I realized I looked as though I was already fading into nothingness.

I must live, at least until my people are safe, and I know they will survive.

I almost laughed.

Even if I did find my true power and return home in time to set the Law aside forever, I would not know if my people would survive. Aidan and Brigit could disappear from the face of the planet, and my people could still die out. No one can stop Mother Earth and Father Sun if they truly wish for us to cease to exist.

"I can see your image has frightened you as much as it has us. We know you have begun to fade."

"Yes, and there is nothing either of us can do about it. The fates have sealed my destiny, and two Death's Heads anticipate my arrival."

I studied my reflection as I told her what had happened. I needed help, and it was time everyone knew. Maybe we could all do something to save my people. From the front seat, Jack and Kyle listened to my every word. I realized this was a way for Kyle to know everything without me breaking my people's trust. He may not understand everything he was about to hear, but at least he would know the entire truth. I used the story to my advantage, and when I had finished with the Death Deities, I started recanting my past. If Jack or Aine knew what I was up to, neither of them had let on. As I spoke, I could hear Jack's sudden intakes of breath, and feel Kyle's erratic driving.

"As a child, I began my tutoring in language skills, including learning to speak and write Latin, Italian, French, Celtic, Gaelic, and English. Father told me then, any future ruler should know how to communicate with all people, at all times. The languages had been chosen, because the Fay had influenced some part of their history. I was also schooled in each of these country's court customs. By the time I became an adult, I could converse and socialize with anyone the Fay had ever influenced.

"My mother spent these years teaching me how to be a good Queen to her people and to her King. She showed me how to be at my King's side whether in court or battle. By her daily activities, she showed me what it meant to be a mother and all it entailed. As you know, my mother was considered a great healer, and she taught me some of her skills.

"When I turned thirty, I was sent to learn how to become a proper wife. I was instructed in the schools of seduction, though since I was future Queen, and not betrothed to any Fay, I was kept pure. It was unusual, to say the least.

"Once I returned home, my Father continued my training in becoming a great ruler and warrior. I was taught the same as any Fay Guard, and Father trained me in swords himself. My mother, at this time, was learning and experimenting in advanced healing arts and trying to get some of our Laws changed.

"On my hundredth birthday, it was announced I was to choose a King and become betrothed. But, Father listened to my whims and allowed me to study the Gods and Goddesses in-depth, more than others were taught. All Fay know the Deities, but only a few, like you and I, Aine, know what can be wrought of such knowledge."

Turning to look at her, I waited for her slight nod before continuing.

"Then, as you know, Mother had a terrible argument with Brigit. Only Mother and Brigit... possibly Aidan, knew what it was about. The following day, Mother called me to her room to say goodbye. It was then that she cast her last chant, her exact words were...

"My wish, however, is for you. I wish for you to find love, my daughter, and not just any love, but a love like your Father's and mine. A love greater than all things and all time. A love to keep you warm on a cold night, to give you light in the bitter darkness, to fill your body and soul when you feel there is no joy left to be had. Your heart's desire, your deepest secret, your sleeping mind's cry, your true love. When you find your true love, let nothing, or no one stand in your way. Let the Gods themselves guide and protect it, while the Goddesses nurture it and tend it, until it overcomes anything and anyone around you. That is the wish, and the last thing I ask. A great love for you, my daughter, greater than any man or woman has ever known."

"It was with those words, I believe, we ended up coming to Kyle's world, for he surely is my mother's wish granted."

I wandered in memories of my Mother, having become so very tired. A covering was put over my chilly body as I waited for their replies, but sleep blissfully overcame me.

Chapter Fourteen

A MOTHER'S RETURN

"Shayla, Shayla! It is time to get up now. Wake to a new day. It is not time for you to fade yet."

My old bones rattled. Mother stood before me, her voice a faint whispering in my head as the ethers surged about her. She wore her favorite white gown. When she moved, the ivory beads in her long, black hair drifted. I blinked.

"It is truly I, Daughter. Now you must awake. You have found your true love, and now you must set everything right in Fay Land. I love you, Daughter. Now...wake up."

I closed my eyes. "I do not wish to wake up. If I wake, you are gone, and father and I are alone."

She shook her head. "Gone from the physical world, but I will never leave you, or your father's heart. Remember, Shayla. Fading is not an end, but merely a passing on to a higher plain. Here I am, surrounded in beauty and can look upon you at any time. Now you must do what is best for you. You must awake and embrace the man trying so desperately to wake you."

The man.

"One more thing. Please tell your father I love and miss him. Now go, and do not fret over my loss anymore. Be happy and live to bring my grandchildren to life."

She waved a hand toward me. I clung to the surreal vision of her long fingers, but whether I wished it or not, my eyes fluttered.

"Shayla... I thought I had..." Kyle's voice choked. His cheeks were wet with tears.

"I am all right. I was speaking to Mother." For a moment I contemplated the hurt in his eyes. "Promise me after I go to the next statue, magic or not, we will spend some time alone before I have to return home. Even if just in shared silence."

"Yes, anything you want."

Fear and adoration shook in his voice, and I knew nothing was to be done for it. We had to live through all this, and maybe survive. Kyle sounded terrified, maybe because he finally realized I was only so much mist, perhaps never to see me again. I did not know of his beliefs in the afterlife. Either way, nothing could be done.

"Princess, are you all right?" Jack's voice echoed from far away. I noticed we were in a hotel room. The dark drapes drawn in front of the window, barely let in any light from what must have been the remainder of the day. The bed I laid on spread out on either side of me, and I could feel a lingering warmth penetrating the indentation next to mine. Someone had spent the night beside me.

"What day is it?"

Aine's face appeared next to Kyle's. "December twenty-first. A little past noon."

"The twenty-first? I slept away two days? How far are we away from Dunvegan?"

149

"We are in Harlosh only about an hour's drive from Dunvegan. I figured we could go straight to the cave once we get there."

I still felt dreary, though better than I had in days. I gained energy, only to lose time. I was still slipping away. "Yes, that is a good idea. On the way, I will tell you what happened in my dream."

They insisted we eat before going. I tried, but all I could manage were small bits of fruit and some bread. My appetite still had not returned, and I tolerated their troubled, anxious glances by smiling and reassuring them. Aine especially could not contain her upset, even after I spoke of what Mother said.

"What does this change?"

"Nothing, I fear, except for the plans going home. Instead of us driving to Cambletown, I think we should hire someone to drive Kyle's truck there and we sail down. Kyle, do you know of anyone you trust enough to take care of your truck?"

"A friend of mine has a boat we can use. He is normally home this time of year. I can leave the truck at his place and sail back with the crew."

His voice dug a dagger in my heart, and I was responsible. "Thank you, Kyle."

I would either die in the human world, leaving my people in the hands of Aidan and Brigit, or I would return home and leave my people in the hands of someone I trusted. I must return home. Did I love my people enough to sacrifice all I am and ever would be? The answer was simply, yes. Nothing, not even my overwhelming need to be with Kyle, would ever change that.

When we arrived in Dunvegan, Kyle drove steadily through the village. I noticed shops of all varieties and wished I could have more time to linger and meet the locals. Once we were through the town, Kyle drove into the surrounding hills.

"The lake is located on the other side of this hill. Once we get there, we'll take a boat to get to the small, center island. It's called Corra's Keep, and the cave is at the middle."

"A middle within a center?" Aine asked. "There must be some reason why the island is in the center of the lake, and the cave in the center of that."

"The local legend is Corra made the cave first, then the island, and finally the lake. It is said she made everything in the center as a reminder of all things having a beginning and touching everything else. Since she is the Goddess of prophecy, most people try not to forget her words."

The myth grew. Corra's lake rippled in waves of a soft and translucent turquoise, clear enough to see the mottled rocks underneath. A grassy perimeter with scattered flowers surrounded the fresh waters. I sensed Aine marveling at the birds, and how the drifting water kept time to their song.

Allowing the jasmine and heather to drift around me, I closed my eyes while picking out and inhaling their sweet aroma. This was a cleansing place, a place to refill an empty soul. Aine and I were not the only ones to be content and amazed. Kyle's breath quickened, while Jack thanked the Goddess for nature's perfect gift. I understood Kyle's revelation. This was where I would receive my gift. I also understood Jack's need to praise the Goddess, for surely her presence was still here, stronger than ever.

Bells chimed a tender whisper on the wind.

"Come to me, Queen Shayla. Come and receive what I have waited so long to give."

"We need to cross the lake now; she is waiting for me."

I pointed to the small, white boat at the edge of the lake. No one questioned its remarkable presence, or my request. They only did as I asked. I climbed in, and once we were seated, Kyle began rowing our way across. I hoped he would go faster, but the rigid line of his back bade me be patient.

Instead, I faced my reflection in the water as it undulated by, contemplating death without fear, knowing that even if this boat were to overturn, a drowning would not stop me from reaching the island.

Somehow, I would always make it. I would become a fish and swim.

On the island, we made our way to the center easily enough. Silver stones and golden sands led us to the cave's entrance. I strode to the sacred opening I knew existed behind its vines of jade and turned to the others before passing through the curtain.

"This is as far as you all can go. I have to go the rest of the way alone."

I swept the ivy aside, and made my way in. Painted cranes of all sizes dotted the walls, each prepared for flight. I turned back once to gaze at the entrance, but there was only blackness.

"Come, Queen of the Fay. I do not wish to wait any longer to give you what I have waited lifetimes to pass on."

Her voice became closer with each step I took. Emerging through a jewel-strewn doorway, I finally bore myself into her presence. Corra wore the appearance of a crane. Incredible, she was as white as snow, and at least ten feet of pure marble.

"Step closer, Daughter of the Gods. Step up and claim your true power, my Child of the Brides."

I was stunned. Only powerful Fay received such a compliment.

"Never doubt what and who you are. You are the future."

"The future? I am fading even now."

I dropped to my knees, trying to catch my breath as the tears came. My people were dying. What could I do?

"Ah, but you see that is where you are wrong. You can and will do something about it. Your heart is pure, your love true, and your magic strong. These are all you need to save our people, and perhaps someone you love. Rise and receive my gift to you."

I lifted myself from the floor, but kept my head lowered.

Of all the Gods and Goddesses, I had seen since coming to this land, I sensed her power and dignity. She deserved my tribute and respect.

"I fear I have nothing to offer you for this gift. My body and spirit have already been claimed. What would you ask of me instead?"

"One of the males you travel with owns your heart. Is this true?"

I hung my head, though I felt no shame. I knew my people should mean more to me. Kyle meant as much.

"Then love him. Really love him. Hold nothing from yourself back. Trust what you feel inside, not what has been pre-approved for your life and heart. Finish your mother's wish. Fulfill it. That is all I want from you."

Nodding, I touch her right wing and felt the warm sea air blow through me, cleansing me, making me whole. The darkness was replaced with heartiness and passion. I was infused with my people's past, and there were no secrets. I heard every Fay's thought as though they were my own. I was truly their Queen in not only words and acts, but in magic as well.

At that moment, they knew it. Some rejoiced, while others doubted what was happening, but two minds cursed, and I knew. I heard what had happened to my mother. Brigit had laced my mother's drink with a special poison, killing the one Fay closest to me. My beloved Mother, and the one person who could have stopped all of her scheming and plotting.

Another voice shocked me. It was Kyle. I could hear his thoughts, feel his obsession. Though I always wondered if he were truly Fay, I knew it now without a doubt. He had always been confused. There had been no one to initiate him in his heritage.

My true power was something buried deep within, always there, but never used properly. It was love for my people. All of them. I sent an image to Fearghus, warning him of what had happened to Queen Gwendolyn, and instructions to detain Brigit where she could not harm anyone until I returned home.

"Now go Shayla, Queen of the Fay. Go to give all you can to the man you love, to your Mother's wish, and to know your people will be safe until you return. Also, if you should have a daughter, you might consider naming her after your Mother and Myself."

I could not suppress a smile as the magic in the cave vanished. The cranes that looked as though they would fly away to the stars were old stains on a deserted black wall. The door of green vines, once an eternal memory of spring, now rustled as wintered leaves. I stepped outside, my cheeks stinging with the cold reminder of winter.

I breathed deep. Corra had saved the last of her earthly powers to bring my gift to the surface. Now, all that was left was a distant reminder of what had been. I looked to Jack and Aine. They felt the loss as deep as I had, but when I gazed at Kyle, he looked worse. The dark circles under his eyes, told of the life drained out of him since I disappeared into the cave.

Did he realize who I now was? Whether I had died or gone on to rule, he was losing. When I reached his side, he looked down at me and sighed. *Could I save you? Would you ask me to save you?*

"This is the end, Shayla."

Puzzled, but patient, I waited for him to go on.

"Do you remember when we met, and I told you I was dying. That is was part of my families curse?"

"Of course. How could I ever forget? It was one of the saddest moments in my life."

"Each time the male of our family has died, something important and foretold has come to pass. My great grandfather watched the island of his beloved sink into the sea. My grandfather suffered when our family castle fell, never to be rebuilt again. My father was foretold of my birth on the day he was to die. As I came into this world, he left it. I was told the Lake of Corra would be no more. I kept watching for some kind of storm, and then, when I knew I had to take you here, I realized it would happen as I stood in the center of it. My birthday falls on the same day as yours. I will be thirty-one the 25th of December. Today finishes what began when my life started. There will be no more after me. I am the last."

159

The world tilted and tried to plummet out from under my feet. This was the reason he wanted to be with Sophie on Christmas, so he would not face his death alone. The knowledge that he would die after I returned, caused a poignancy in my chest that threatened to consume me, and my responsibility. There was no way I could save my people and return in time to try and save him.

"Now, no tears. I have known for a very long time I would die and when. My only regret is not to have had more time with you. Come on, we need to get back across the lake and to the port before it gets much darker."

I looked up and saw the skies with their gloomy cast. How much time had passed inside the caves while they were possessed of magic was hard to predict. But the proof of altered time had never been more noticeable than now. Time provoked me with his power and hurried me along.

Chapter Fifteen

TWO DAYS LEFT

Once we had reached the docks, Kyle introduced us to his friend Mack, who was nowhere near as tall, and owned a proud head of bright red hair, complimenting a pale, freckled skin. Leprechaun blood. I smiled as Kyle introduced us.

"Hello. My Sophie has told me all about you. She was only sorry she did not get a proper chance to meet the woman who had won Kyle's heart."

I had the grace to blush. Not for the kind word, but for my unforgivably bad behavior.

"Please give her my most sincere apologies, and let her know, if I should ever return, I will pay her a proper call. I hate to seem pushy, but we really should be heading out. From what I understand, the trip will take two days instead of one."

"Yes ma'am. We normally do not use this route unless absolutely necessary. Don't you be worrying none, the crew can handle Spit Fire and any seas blown her way." His smiling eyes and mouth rolled upwards at my uncertainty. "Spit Fire... schooner. And a very specially built schooner. Large and able."

He winked. "She be named after Sophie, and the first we met. 'Tis a long story. When you return, I will explain. She will very much appreciate the telling as much as I."

Mack grinned, as a young lad ambled up to him. "We're ready to head out, sir."

"That sounds like us," Kyle said. "Come on, Aine, Jack. I'll show you where you'll spend the next two days."

He led them onto the boat, and I turned back to the captain. "I want to thank you again, for lending us Spit Fire."

"It is no need. Kyle is my best friend. If you wish the repayment, try and make his last few days on Earth pleasant."

He winked as my mouth gaped. It was no use attempting to cover my shock at his knowing Kyle's fate. The fact he had asked me to keep his friend happy did not even register, until he deposited me over the starboard and walked away. I fingered the note he had pressed into my hand, watching his steady back retreat. When I finally read his words, I laughed.

'The Captain of Spit Fire is able to marry people.'

Well, at least I knew how he wanted me to make Kyle happy. I thought of Aine and Jack. If we returned home, and my fate came to pass anyway, I had decided there was no one better for the Fay than them. If they chose to marry, there would be nothing to stop me from making them Queen and King.

Lost in my newest thought, I did not sense Aine coming up behind me.

"Shayla, can I ask you something privately please?"

"Of course. What is it?"

163

"I wondered if there was any way Jack and I could remain here in the human's world? He and I wish to marry, and I do not know if my family would consent."

This was something I had not considered. "I will not force you to return home, but I will ask you to answer a few questions."

"Indeed, my Queen."

"So, you accepted my call. If you and Jack are married now, would you both be willing to return home?"

"You must know how I feel. I would never give up my family or home if I had any other choice. I know Jack would not like to leave his mother behind. Yes, if he and I could be married, we would return."

"Do you not agree, I have the power and authority to approve your marriage?"

"I had not the daring to ask, considering you cannot be with the man you love."

"There is no more worry. I shall grant you and Jack my permission, and I have heard it on great authority, the captain of this vessel can perform the ceremony. So, my dear friend, I think you should go and tell Jack the good news, then find the captain and start making the plans. The only stipulation is we must have you wed and a couple before we reach our destination."

Aine ran from me, and I felt a charged spark of envy gather in my chest.

No!

I would not be jealous of them because they found love. Taking in a cleansing breath, I closed my eyes and allowed the cool sea breeze to refresh my face, as the boat undulated with a purpose beneath me.

"Why so solemn? There will be a marriage celebration at midnight."

"Midnight? That was quick." I leaned against Kyle.

I am doing what is best for my people. I am returning home to my imminent death, leaving the man I love behind to die alone. I knew, no matter how fast the boat travels, I will not make it to either Sophie's or your home in time.

"Tell me out loud what is wrong."

"I am wishing a spell for time."

"You still believe you will die when you return home?"

I shrugged. "As far as I know, nothing has changed."

"If both of us are to die within a matter of days, why do we not make the best of the time we have left?"

His eyes twinkled and I could not hold back the laughter rising in me. "I will have to help Aine with the wedding, but afterwards, I am yours to do with as you choose."

"I will hold you to that. I might as well help Jack."

Kyle's hand nestled in mine, as we walked to the couple's room. Corra's boon was already making things seem easier. At least I could forget for a few hours. Aine paced and chattered, while dots of sweat covered Jack's neck. They had only known each other more intimately the last few days, and now they were being betrothed. I wondered of the wisdom in speaking my decision aloud, choosing them as my successors. Both had proven, over and over, their devotion to the Fay and the ability to learn and lead.

"What will my family and our people say of our marriage?" Aine asked. "What of the Fay part of the ceremony?"

"We will see," I responded. She looked to me, like others would look to her. She would be a fine Queen.

Kyle and I engaged the nervous couple until the time arrived. After the captain had pronounced them man and wife, he and the crew disappeared into the dining room to await the wedded couple's arrival.

"Now that we are alone, I will perform my part of the ceremony." The slight wind was cool, as I bound their hands together with a small bit of cloth I had fashioned. "May Anu, Mother Earth, and Lugh, Father Sun, guide and protect you and your children. May the

Goddess Corra bless each day of your lives together. Let no man or woman break what the Gods themselves have wrought this night."

As I tightened the bond, I sensed a piece of their future blessed with children. I knew not where they lived, but I knew they were happy, and at least a few of the Fay had survived. "I would present now, the future Queen and King of Fay."

"My Queen?" Jack asked. His small, private smiles to me had been apologies for his behavior. We did not need to speak of it. I was joyful he lived this moment, relieved and happy. His boyhood infatuation with me was better fashioned on Aine. She would thrive on his protection.

"I am not assured of my fate, or those of our people, but I do know there are no two I would trust more with keeping our people safe. I announce to you, the Fay, and any Deities listening, my choice of Aine and Jack of the Fay, to be King and Queen of Fay upon my death."

There was a deep trembling from the water. The tremor passed into the boat, to our feet, and for a brief moment, the boat felt as if it would shiver apart. I looked up for the sign. The moon, bearing her fullness earlier, was now half. My breath caught. Divided. Well, I care not one whit what they think. I am Queen here. I am the decision maker.

Either way, the Fay world shifted once more. It would be up to Aine and Jack to be strong enough to survive it and guide our people to a new way of life.

Kyle and I followed the stunned couple to the dining room where the crew had thrown together a celebration. Aine and I were the only women aboard, and each of the crew had a turn dancing. Well into sunrise, Aine finally begged to be allowed to rest. The crew laughed and teased, bowing repeatedly to the bride and groom as they made their way out.

"I think it is time for us to retire also." Kyle grabbed my hand and led me to our cabin.

"I love you," I said, as we entered the room.

"And I love you. How about a shower and some rest?"

For once, it was not what I had in mind, but I knew he was right. I was exhausted, and I knew he had to be more so. I was not sure what had bumped me, but I sat in my bedroom on Fay Island. Fearghus hurried through the door, frowning and breathing as though every rise of his chest were his last. I thought to greet him, and began to rise, when I felt the chains upon my hands and ankles. I pulled at the bindings and turned, confused and hurt, toward him. I hope he realized that I was not truly there yet.

"I fear, my Queen, the worst has been decided. They have ordered the death of you and the human babe you carry."

"Fearghus! I am not truly here. This is just another dream. Babe! What babe are you talking about?"

"The babe you and the human escort created. I am afraid this is no dream. I have known each time whether you were dreaming. Is that not true?"

I hesitated. Was I truly home and my people were going to execute me?

"What happened to Aine and Jack? Where are they?"

"No one knows. When you announced your wish for them to take over the throne, an alarm went out to bring the two of them forward. You should have realized the Fay would never allow you to choose your predecessor. They were supposed to be guarding you, when you conceived. It is enough for them to receive the same punishment as you."

He was right. I should have known they would be implicated by a few in some scheme. But what had happened? How did I return home without even knowing it, and when did I become pregnant?

"I am trying to understand, but I need more information. How did I come to be here without even remembering it? Why is the last few days a blank, and what day is it?"

"You have no memory of coming home? This is unexpected. What is the last thing you remember?"

"What day is it?"

"It is your birthday."

"Aine and Jack were married on the boat. We were traveling to the Fay waiting to bring us home. We had just finished the celebration, and Jack and Aine had gone to their room. I even blessed the marriage and waited for a sign. Kyle and I retired to the cabin. He suggested I take a shower. It is the last thing I remember."

"You sound as though you have been drugged. The Fay know of your power, but it has not swayed their decision. If we could establish your innocence by proving the deceit, they would have to reconsider. You could not rule Fay, but you might be spared. We must find out when you were drugged."

I stared as though he had lost his mind. Not be allowed to rule my people? How could they even decide such a thing? They decided on execution.

"We need to test and find out what drug was used. We might even be able to prove you were not in your own mind when you consented to the human. I will start the process. If anyone comes to get you, ask them for your last request. Say anything that will take a few hours." Fearghus left the room.

I tried to remember what had happened, calling on magic to ease the blinders in my mind, but nothing would come.

"What now?"

I almost did not recognize it, when I received an answer.

"What do you want?" Corra asked carefully.

"I want to know what happened to me. I want to be back on the boat with Kyle spending our last days together, showing him how much I love him and will never spend a moment not thinking about him."

"You do not wish to be Queen of your people, to live and rule for centuries to come?"

Trick question. I did not care if I got it right or not.

"No, I want to be with the man I love for whatever time we have."

"So be it, but know I could fix all of this. You would be Queen of Fay, and the child you will eventually carry, would follow in your footsteps. Is being with him worth the life of your child?"

I paused and thought hard. I hoped my child would forgive me. "If Kyle is the father, then do you not think I should be there when we created it? As it is now, I do not feel as though any part of him is with me."

"It is well you know your body. You are right, there is no child there, only a malevolent spell. I shall return you to him, but it will be the following evening. It is all I can do."

I nodded my head as the outside of my vision starting to blur. The next I knew; I was looking up into three pairs of concerned eyes.

"Shayla. Sweetheart, are you all right?"

"Fine. Tired, is all."

I was not going to tell them, but I would not allow Aine and Jack to return home with me. They would be with Kyle when he died. Kyle wanted to question me, his face contorted, sensing there might be an emergency, and Aine frowned. Jack, my old pro-active friend, knew I was lying. He sensed the crisis and chose to keep silent. Most likely he had not yet figured out what to do exactly.

"I do not know about the rest of you," Jack said, "but I am famished. I say we share dinner together, before retiring for the night."

We agreed, and I waved them to go on ahead without me, explaining I needed to freshen up first. None of them liked the idea, but did as I asked. Once alone, I grabbed a quick shower and let the surge relax me, so I could think over what had happened. I was going to return home carrying a human child, either Kyle's or another's. I was not positive, but surely, I knew whom it would belong to. The Gods were tricky. Aidan would be the only one brave or stupid or lucky enough to pull off such a stunt. It made me wonder how far ahead his plans were laid. I was sure of one thing concerning Aidan, though. I would not give him a chance.

Grabbing a bottle of Fay wine, I had packed deep in my bags, I headed toward the dining room. Jack, Aine and Kyle talked as I entered.

"Aine, I do love her, but we have very little time left. This is all we will ever have. I am willing to spend this last night with her, and let go when the time comes. I may never be able to hold her in my arms, but she will forever be in my heart. I will die knowing her love, and it is all I could have ever wanted or asked for."

I strode up to Kyle. "And I love you and shall treasure our time together for all eternity." Taking his hand in mine, I led him to one of the tables waiting for us.

It was time promised. Kyle poured the heady wine, and we drank while eating roasted chicken and potatoes, enjoying each other's presence with kind words penetrating the silence. I did not question the rich food; I only thanked the Goddess. Pouring the precious wine into bowls, we ate cake and strawberries. If anyone wondered at my use of the wine, no one commented. I did not wish to be in their heads at the moment.

Once dinner was done, I ordered some of the strong tea the sailors loved to drink, and used magic and the wine as added flavor. We danced to soft Celtic music. I saw the worry and homesickness in Aine and Jack's eyes.

What I would tell them would hurt, but there was no other way.

Kyle finally excused us, and we went back to our cabin. The door barely had time to shut before he pulled me to him. "I feel as though I have waited a lifetime for this. No more dreams. No more waiting. You are mine tonight, and no one is going to stop us."

There were no more words. He pulled at my dress until it slipped over my head, and gasped. Men were funny about clothes. He did not expect me to be wearing only panties. I may be Queen, but I was foremost woman. The dress provided the convenience of not needing to remove too many clothes, and I had chosen it especially for tonight.

Kyle did not hesitate. His strong hands traveled up my sides and cupped my breasts, and circling them until my nipples were squeezed between his nimble fingers. He plucked at them like a finely tuned Lyre, until I thought they could not become more unyielding.

As his head reached down to suckle me, I whimpered. My breasts pleaded and responded, the sensation of his wet tongue sending shivers of fire down my spine and through my legs.

My knees buckled, and he lifted me to his hips. Through his clothes, he pulsed against me, hard and ready. I responded, our bodies clicking rhythmically like a clock towards timelessness. Neither of us could control it, it just kept on, wanting to flow for eternity.

He balanced me against the cabin wall, and with a fierce growl, ripped my panties from my hips. Sensuously, slowly, he held me pressed, naked, circling his hips and rubbing his cock against me... caressing my inner thighs, the crook of my inner hip, the heated animal that wished to devour him between my legs. I needed him... it... more than anything. As Kyle suckled my breast, he spread his legs far enough to release one hand, and caress it between our bodies, touching me. With each draw of his mouth, he stroked my swollen clitoris, bringing the need for rapture within me stronger and higher. Just when I thought he would break me, he slowly pulled his mouth from my breast, and tongued his way to the other, his hand resting, cupping me below.

Sweet Goddess of Torture.

My heart slowed and he began again, pulling me between his fingers and mouth one second, and the next, speeding once or twice over my other breast and the saturated flesh existing between my thighs. With each stroke, I began to fall over the edge of bliss, but he kept pulling back until he had me weeping for release. When Kyle could take it no longer, he pushed us away from the wall with a heave, and carried me to the bed. I knew what he would do.

No.

I disengaged from him, and pushed him over and down, straddling him in one easy movement. I was confident he understood, and we smiled. I kept up our game of silence, arching an eyebrow at him, before lowering my mouth to his neck, daring him to stop me. I flicked my tongue at one tiny spot at a time, covering each part of the salty, musky morsel beneath me. Satiated, I made new travels down his pliant body, one flicker at a time, stopping to tease his nipples one after the other. As I moved my way down his steely abdomen, he grabbed me roughly under the arms and threw me under him, pinning me.

The same arching eyebrow greeted me. In a game of competition, he engaged his teeth on my jawbone and neck, while his hands explored me, exploring every fleshy curve I had. I was his finely tuned machine, wet and ready to perform. His fingers teased me from the outside and penetrated me within, first one, then with two. I pushed my hips down, succumbing to the game, letting him undo me. Before I could take my next breath, I no longer stood on the edge of flight, but took off.

He pierced me in one stroke. I was broken, no longer a virgin and Kyle was my bane, my God. He paused as I reveled in my new state and it's fullness. Not breaking our vow of silence, and to show him everything was good in the world, I thrust my hips. He growled and pinned his against mine, showing he maintained domination. Slowly, he moved, each shift of his pelvis precise. When I thought I had caught his rhythm, he would change it, taking control all over again. I did not mind being at his mercy, he was faultless and loved me.

What else do I need?

There were no worries or responsibilities. I succumbed to him and his authority and treasured it. He was fierce and demanding. Each time he plunged into me, my whimpers became moans, which became shouts and screams. He gasped in male bliss and pushed us farther, harder.

I was crushed. Each quiver of my orgasm was finished by his body's pulsating response, over and over. I sensed the life exploring and searching inside of me. The intensity of our lives, in that small moment, I knew we created a child.

Lying entwined, our breaths slowed to their individual paces. Kyle withdrew and picked me up, heading for the bathroom. There was a shower for two on one wall, and a spa against the other. I was amazed at human bathroom magic.

"The head, sweetheart, the head." Kyle's smile should have broken his face. "Shower or bath?"

"Oh...bath. I do not think I could stand long enough for a shower."

Chuckling, he placed me on the towel lying across the edge of the tub, and turned on the taps. "You know, this could take a few minutes. Are you sure you do not want the shower instead?"

"Positive. Besides, what is the difference? Ten- or fifteen-minutes tops?"

"Maybe less, if I know Mack. More than likely, he increased the water pressure for this thing. While we wait, you want to tell me what that look was for earlier?"

"I was surprised, is all. I guess I had not completely understood what us making love in the dreams meant. I knew they were special and a waking dream, but I never realized what happens in them affecting life as such."

"Want to explain that a little better?"

"In normal dreams, what happens in them, does not affect you in real life. But the dreams we have shared together affect me. I realize you may not believe it, but this was my first. Yet, when you entered me, my maidenhead did not break. It was already gone."

"You remember the falls correct. When we made love in them, I felt it then. I have been able to walk in others dreams, but never like when I am with you. I can sense things with you."

"I know why. What happens between us in the dreams is real. The first time we were both awake, but each time after that, I was asleep. Somehow, what happened in the pool placed a connection between us that now blurs the lines of dreams and reality."

"The tub's ready."

I stepped into the warm water, not sure why Kyle had changed the subject, but I let him. It gave me time to think through telling him about the child we created. It only took me a moment to realize, telling him would add an extra burden upon his shoulders when he faced his death. There would be nothing either he or I could do about it.

"Will you let me wash your hair?"

"Do you think I would actually say no? I am forced by my people's custom to keep it at least this long, but there are more times than I can count, I wished I could cut it off."

"So... your people are real Fay, huh? I guess they have pretty strict rules?"

"Yes, there is strictness, but not as much as you might think. Being a Princess and future ruler, grants me the privilege of having a few more liberties than others." An explosive snigger escaped my lips. I surprised myself. I could joke about my life and not be sarcastic or melancholy.

Fearghus would disagree. I smiled.

"Hey! I think that's the first time I ever heard you make a joke. Not a very good one, but still a joke."

I punched at him, and he recoiled in the pretense I had knocked him off the side of the tub. I came up and swung again. Catching my arm, he laughed, as I attempted to show him, I was his warrior queen. He feinted, before pulling me to his chest and kissing me thoroughly.

"Now that I have your attention, would you please turn around so I can wash this beautiful head of hair?"

He got in with me, and I did as he asked, not regretting it for one moment. He was more thorough than I ever was. I relaxed and closed my eyes, contemplating my hair would be clean for at least the next week. I dipped beneath the water, rinsing my head of bubbles, as he fondled my body with the bar of soap. I was aroused again.

Standing, dripping water everywhere, I pulled Kyle out of the tub and led him to the rug on the floor. We would have need of a dry bed when the night was through. I pushed him down to his back, and maneuvered my body on top of his. He helped me guide him in me and we agreed on a slow, heart-wrenching pace. This climax was a sweet completion of our love. With tears rolling down my face, I bent over and placed my lips against his.

"I love you, Kyle. May the Gods be merciful and allow us, to meet again."

"And I love you my Shayla, Queen of Fay." He wiped the tears from my face before hugging me fiercely.

I do not think either of us was ready for the night to end, but we both knew each other needed sleep before the morrow. In regretful alliance, we climbed once more into the huge bed and clutched each other tightly, finally drifting off to sleep.

Fearghus appeared that night, staring down at Kyle and me. I stood next to him and looked down at us. Looking to Fearghus, I saw something flicker in his eyes.

"My Queen, I fear I have more bad news."

"Is it worse than before?"

"The council has discovered your love for this man, and is furious. I fear, if you had not already arrived deceased, they would have demanded your life on the spot. As it is now, they are deciding on whether or not to allow your body onto the island for you to fade." Fearghus' looked skeletal in the strange shadows of our meeting. I realized then it was a reflection of his heart's horror.

"Will the guards be waiting for us at Rathin Island?"

"They are waiting for you at Cambletown."

So, time had changed, again. "How did I die this time?"

"No one knows for sure, but it is believed you were strangled by a human. The guards said you had welts around your neck when they found you."

Not only have things changed, but one of my own people will kill me. Surely the Elders realize no mortal man could kill me and it had to be a Fay. But who? The only real benefit from my death goes to Brigit and Aidan, and Aidan wants me for my body and the crown. Unless he realizes I have my powers now, and knows that he can never have me.

"The elders and the rest of Fay know I have my power?"

"Yes, it was quite an energy burst throughout the island. There is not a plant, animal, or Fay who did not feel its effects."

"You know as well as I do, no ordinary mortal could have killed me, it was a Fay. You also know who would benefit the most from having me killed."

"Brigit, but not Aidan. He was furious when he found out he could not have you. Even if you had been with this man. He wants the crown, but he wants you even more. I am confident of it. He even admitted to the Elders that he had considered drugging you to get you pregnant with his child."

"What? He admitted it? Goddess Corra save us."

"So, what will we do now?"

"I am going to get up and not wake Kyle. I will see about getting off this boat and turning it around. Hopefully, I can surprise the guards at the port. You are going to send trusted guards to meet me at Islay instead. Can you do that?"

"Yes, we have the portal in Islay. I will have them meet you at the docks and bring you back here. We will hide you until a way is found to save you, and our misled people."

I nodded, then forced my body to wake up. Kyle did not move as I crawled out of the bed to scoop up my dress, sandals, and the bag I would need. The door was silent, and the hall lights dimmed, just enough to see by. I glided my way to the public head, my nakedness symbolic. It freed me to become the Queen of Fay. No one saw me. Using my magic, I became the Queen of Spies.

Once I was dressed, I made my way up to the deck. I knew it was risky going to the captain's cabin, but I did not have time to find a safer way. Placing my hands on one part of the boat, then the next, I felt my way around deck, sensing the nighttime and its sleeping inhabitants. A deckhand stirred. The moon greeting me with her insomnia, and I thanked the Goddess Cerridwen for casting her glow.

The captain's door was locked. Feeling my nerve starting to slip, I rapped erratically before I could convince myself otherwise. The sound echoed in my ears. I hoped it sounded a natural creak in the wind.

I was proud I did not jump when the echo responded gently on my shoulder. Turning, I was greeted by a shadowy face surrounded by a mass of red hair. He is not so sleepy, after all.

"I need to speak with you privately, captain."

"I was heading up to the helm to give a break. If you want, we can talk there."

"That would be perfect."

I waited until the room was clear before heading inside.

"What can I do for you?"

"I need to get off at Islay, instead of Cambletown."

"I will clear it with Kyle first, but I do not see a problem with that."

"No. No one can know, but you and me. If we sail to Cambletown, they will be hurt. Probably your crew along with them. Jack and Aine are very close to me, and I love Kyle. Please. Help me to save them."

"You speak of danger. I would know the why and how. Who will be waiting there? The men are not afraid of a scrap, and the harbor police are in the port."

"Yes, but you must believe me when I say there is nothing, they can do to stop this. As far as who or how, you would not believe me, and I have not the time to explain. Will you please just listen to me for the love of Manannan? Please, just do as I ask?"

I was not sure if it was what I said, or how I said it, but he nodded his head in agreement. "When we drop you off, what do you suggest we do after?"

"It is a few days till Yule. Go home to be with your family and loved ones. I do not know how you will keep the others from finding out what has happened. You most likely will not be able to. Just please take care of them."

He nodded. "We dock in Islay in thirty minutes."

I spent the time writing goodbye letters.

Aine,

I know this is hard to understand, but you and Jack must not return to Fay Island unless Fearghus or I come to get you. Things have changed drastically, and if you return, you will both die. I want to thank you for being there, and for being my friend. May you and Jack live happily ever after. Know that the children you will birth, are beautiful and healthy. Please be with Kyle when his time comes, and tell him I love him as he passes from this world to the next.

I consider you a true friend.

Shayla.

I wrote a similar letter to Jack and told him I would have Fearghus make sure his mother was taken care of. Kyle's letter was the shortest and hardest of all three.

Kyle,

I love you. I am sorry I had to leave you this way. Goodbye my love.

Shayla.

When we reached Islay, I handed Mack the letters and made my way off the Spit Fire. He waved a silent goodbye, before turning the boat to Dunvegan. Pulling one of Kyle's sweaters from my bag, I inhaled his scent before slipping it over my head. I stood for several moments in the early dawn crying softly, I knew I would never see Kyle again.

Chapter Sixteen

THE HIDDEN WAY HOME

"Queen Shayla?"

Startled, I turned to find a Fay guard standing behind me. Silent as the night, I sensed his impression in the darkness.

"Yes..."

"Fearghus sent me. He said to tell you, I was the only one he could trust to keep you safe and guide you through the portal."

"Thank you. I am ready if you are."

"Yes, Queen."

We made our way to the hidden doorway, as I studied his sleek back. "I am sorry, but I do not seem to recall meeting you."

"That is good, but you have seen me. There was a time you fell into the waterfall pool and could not swim. The second time was the day your mother passed. I am sorry for your loss; she was a great lady."

I was silent. Something inside of me fumbled at the obstacle that lay outside as he spoke.

"I live in the mortal world, off and on. Probably for over 200 years now."

"So that is why you are not as strict on certain protocols as you should be? Do you have a wife?"

"She is a mortal, and we have three small girls."

How is that possible?

"I have been around since before your grandfather changed the Law, and when he did, I was considered too valuable in this world to abandon."

He can read my thoughts.

"Because I am a guard of the old royal blood. My family has always read thoughts projected to us by the King or Queen of Fay."

Since you can read my thoughts, why not show me how to read yours?

"I am sorry, my Queen, but unless you were born with the gift, I cannot teach you how to use it."

*Oh, that is a handy bit of power to have over
the King and Queen.*

"Indeed."

I shored up my energies, and we spent the rest
of the walk in silence. I had too many other problems
to think about. Using power to ask questions, having
nothing to do with events as they sped to their ugly
conclusions, was something I pushed to the side. If I
were in danger, I would deal with it at that moment.
Unless some miracle happened, I would die anyway,
and my people would be lost.

"We are here. All you have to do is walk
through the shadow between the white stone and oak
tree, and you will be in Fay."

I looked toward the shadow he was speaking of,
and wondered at the simplicity of it. *How did it keep
anyone or anything from wandering through it?*

"This doorway is for Fay only. It senses the
birth and blood. Nothing, or no one else, can pass the
checkpoint without it. The sun must also be at a
certain angle, or the shadow will not be in the correct

197

location. You must hurry. It will only last a few seconds longer, and will not be back until this time tomorrow."

I gaped at him. What planet, exactly, did he live on? It was yet night.

"The sun on the other side of the earth, Queen."

"Of course." I muttered.

There are too many things I am unaware of.

I did not allow him to respond, but took him at his word and walked toward the portal. I realized I had not asked his name, as a steady current of wind hit my chin. The edge of the door vibrated.

Gabe.

The name resonated through my mind. I knew I had not read Gabe's thoughts, per se, I had simply plucked the information from the essence surrounding him. *Why would he tell me I could not read his mind, if it was possible?*

"He told you, unless you had been born with the gift, it would not matter. The mind is expansive, and the fact that you could read Gabe, is a surprise to me. And I imagine to yourself, as well."

Fearghus stood before me in a room I had never seen before. Surprisingly not shocked by the fact that he had read my thoughts.

"Where are we?"

"My private study. Only two know of this door's existence, now three. You will be safe in here for now. When the Guards report you missing, we may have problems. I would imagine the Elders will make sure you have not already arrived, so they will demand a full search of the Island. When that time comes, there is an alcove hidden above your head.

Perhaps they will not find you there. I will try to be on the team that looks for you here, but I cannot guarantee anything."

"I understand. Do you know if anything has changed since you came to me last night?"

"Not that I know of. Your body will not be found. I do not know what will come after that. Some will suspect magic."

"And what news do you have of my father?"

"He has isolated himself in his private quarters, and refuses to see anyone. I know you want to go to him, but you cannot, the risk is too high. Even now, they anticipate your arrival and sense something wrong."

"So soon? I just got here, and the boat should not arrive until tonight."

"My Queen, I have forgotten to tell you an important fact about using certain doorways. You lose a full day in time. It is the day before your birthday."

"My birthday? Oh, Gods. Fearghus, I did not lose only one day, but two."

He paused as though he had remembered something important. "Yes. The time here, and in the mortal realm, there is difference each time I visit... I am sorry my Queen, but I have done you wrong again. The Gods work as they will. When you came through the doorway, it held you until you were in time with Fay Island."

"Fate's time."

"Yes, my Queen. I must hurry before they suspect anything." He reached out and above me. "Pull on this rock, just there... it will release the latch. You should wait until I have gone from the room. The lights will go out, so I suggest you keep your hand upon it. This room may be soundproof, but I fear the others are not. I do not know if opening doors, magic or otherwise, will make a difference. We can take no chances."

And with that, he was gone.

Chapter Seventeen
CROWNING OUR NEW QUEEN

I silenced myself by lacing my fingers into intricate knots, not paying heed to the dread of something going wrong until Fearghus had a chance. It would be several minutes before the lights were out. I spent the time contemplating and exploring the short climb and its stony niche. It was clean, dry, and as dark as a grave.

Feeling my way, I settled on a cushioned stool and felt one inconspicuous crack letting in a waft of fresh air. It lured my senses, and my eyes played games, making me believe I could see the beating of the walls as if they were alive. Grayness passed through the black, and I realized it was my own subconscious magic, affording me a small reassurance.

I thought of moving out of the black and into the depressing dim, but chose to remain. If someone found the alcove, they would look over there first.

Part of me felt insulted for hiding in my own home, but I knew it was for the best. I had to make it through the day. Everything would change after that, and either I would live, or I would not.

I was not sure how long I had been hiding, but I thought to eat. My body did not call with hunger pangs, but the act would keep my physical energy up. I felt inside my bag for the bread I had taken from Fearghus' table. Finding the plunder, I nibbled like a mouse in the dark. My ears strained for sound, and it took a few minutes before I distinguished real movement and muffled voices. I dared not approach the door, and instead, lay my head against the floor. There was too much stone between us to hear.

The part of me cowering was relieved. If I could not hear them, I would not know. I could live my life a hermit here, stealing scraps from Fearghus' table. At least they should not hear me.

The other part of me knew this was against me. I have never been in a real battle of survival, but I understood the element of surprise was a major factor in a good attack.

The muffled sounds grew faint, and I hoped they left. I knew Fearghus anticipated me hiding until after my birthday. Which may or may not save my life. And my people would be left in the hands of Brigit.

Brigit!

That, I would not allow. Taking a deep breath, I opened my eyes. The light I knew would be there, lanced like a yawning splinter to my right foot. I arose and peered through the crack. Nothing was disturbed. I wondered where the voices had come from and where they went. It was too much. I pushed against the latch, swung open the access, and climbed down just as the door to the room opened.

"I see hoping you would remain hidden was a futile endeavor, and I am surprised you lasted for the hours you have. Be that as it may, and as I make plans, they are changed forever by outside events. Flexibility is an ally. There is a need to reveal yourself. Your father has taken a turn for the worse and fades, so Brigit uses the opportunity to take over the throne. She is choosing her new King at this moment. I brought your ceremonial gown."

"I have known Father was going to die. He did not want to live without Mother, but how will we stop Brigit?"

"Your Father is still King, and his rules must be upheld. You have returned to us with your true power as he instructed. You are the right arm of the Law. You will simply take his place on the throne."

Yes. I knew he was right. He always knew the answer. I would mourn father's passing, when my people were as safe and sane as I could make them. My life for theirs, I cannot stay buried. It was all or nothing.

"None of our lives are more important than the entire Fay. I have no choice now. I do not know if you can do anything about it, but I am carrying Kyle's child. Kyle is also dying, and I believe my death shall come soon. If there is any way to save the babe, will you please try to do so? I owe it to Kyle and his family to try and save their last. Even if the baby is a boy, and he will surely be cursed to death at thirty years of age, you must live long enough to try and save him. Discover the curse and allow him to live."

Fearghus frowned with frustration, but I also saw something that surprised me. Beneath his shock and confusion, existed a seed of anguish. But, before I had time to reason or probe further, he pulled himself up.

"I will do my best; you need not worry. Now, you must hurry. It is almost midnight, and Brigit will not wait for the sun to rise. I will be there as soon as I can. I have a plan, but it may take some time. They will not pass any judgment on you until I arrive."

I did not know what he was up too, but I had grown to trust him. I nodded, as he disappeared through another concealed doorway. How many secrets does Fearghus hold on to? I ran my fingers against the soft fabric of the dress and its attached robe, tears forming in the corners of my eyes. Mother and I had spent weeks making it.

"Fit for a Queen, Shayla. Fit for a wedding."

The gown was made of white silk with satin straps, and fit as well as it had moons ago. Like Kyle's gentle hands, it curved beneath my breasts and cupped them gently. The bodice caressed and accentuated the smallness of my waist.

Throwing the voluminous skirts aside, I slipped on the satin heels, and wound ribbons about my ankles to practice my walk. I needed to declare a regal and authoritarian manner, not one of sentimentality or daintiness. I would outshine any who dared to compete. It was part of the psychology. The gauzy lace and tiny diamonds sewn into the bell-shaped skirt shimmered.

Mother had been right. The large mirror revealed an angel with black hair cascading off her shoulders and down her back, like a robe of tribute.

I covered my head with a long swatch of lace, and secured the crown over it. It was quite different from the simple ring of gold I wore. Crafted of silver and multi-hued sapphires, it was the only color I would wear this day. The gems dipped about my head, dancing on invisible threads. Even the ones encrusted within the crown had a life of their own, begging to be set free.

I finished with my mother's silver and gold sword, placing it inside the white leather sheath and strapping it to my waist.

Once more, the mirror spoke of the truth. An avenging angel. There was nothing left. I tilted my chin up. The mirror is the greatest deceiver. My nervous rattling will now dazzle them all.

Better suited to protect babes, I forced the girl inside of me to the pits of my stomach, and walked out of the room. The hallways seemed deserted, but I knew a malevolent presence advanced. I drew my sword as Aidan strode around the corner. He was not going to stop me.

He stared. "I do not, nor have I ever wished, your harm. I want you very much alive and breathing. I do not know how you discovered my plans, or whether you sensed something, but I must admit, I was very disappointed when your ship did not reach Cambletown."

"You drugged me."

"Then you must know my mother is announcing her new King. I should have known I could not trust that witch. So, you see, my dear Shayla, neither of us have any choice but to ally ourselves against her."

I had a choice. Not one I could use just yet, but I did have one. I would not tell Aidan though. So, he thought we could put the past behind us, and ally ourselves together? I craved to tell him how foolish I thought he was, but knew I could use him to my benefit. He would become my shield and safeguard.

"I agree. Your mother must be stopped, and you will now follow my lead. If you try anything, I will put you out of her misery myself." Aidan's face reddened. "Do you understand?"

I am your only hope, you evil chimera.

"Do not get too used to telling me what to do. I will not be a subservient King."

I let him live in his fantasies. His assumptions bolstered my nerve. Asserting myself once more, I reinforced my skin with an armor of steel, and allowed Aidan to take my arm.

"Keep your friends close, and your enemies closer..." I smirked at Fearghus.

Aidan and I walked arm in arm into the crowded throne room. The gasps greeting us in waves were just as suddenly silenced. As we advanced, the people parted to make way.

Brigit sat on my Father's throne, sifting through eligible bachelors like a harlot selecting a sweet. I spared her a glaring eye to look at the men she had chosen.

Goddess of love, save us.

Draped in gauzy loincloths, several men stood bared to the room. The Fay held no attitudes against the natural forms of nudity in its proper place. The beauty of the naked body was to be worshipped, but this was scandalous and vulgar.

Why do the Fay accept this? They revel in my death; yet accept this whore as their Queen.

Brigit looked up from her wicked contemplation. I was a blaze of glory, angry and disgusted as I advanced toward her. Perhaps I should have concealed my hatred, but it was not to be. I simply could not.

"Seize her." Brigit stood and her voice roared throughout the room. The guards hesitated.

So. Not all would accept a derelict queen...I forced my voice to a higher timbre than hers. "I have returned from the lesser, mortal world with my true power. All in this room know it to be true. My Father, the King, decreed, if I returned before my birthday, I was to take my rightful place as Queen. This is also known to be true. Do you allow a harlot on the throne instead?"

They stirred, their mental murmurs hitting me. There were no denials, and more than a few waves of disgust and abeyance, but I sensed a cowering and darkness. It would seem my people turned their lives towards an obscene bet, swayed by whoever seemed the mightiest. Perhaps life had become dreary with a goalless future. Sometimes a Law steered the people wrong.

"Today is Yule and my birthday. As such, I will take what is rightfully mine."

Several of the men in line bowed to me.

"That may be true," Brigit commented sarcastically, "however, human lover, you must choose a Fay male before you can assume your role. Could you? It would seem you cannot, and once I am wed upon death of your Father, I can assure you, you will not." She waved her hand. "As you can see, I have chosen many."

She triumphed. In my mind, the thing I could not do, was believe she had admitted to scheming whatever it took to keep me from the throne. Brigit polluted herself.

"I am not yet passed." My Father's voice shot from behind the throne. With Aidan on my heels, I advanced up the steps to the throne, and turned to see him in the entryway. Two guards flanked King Domhnall wearing the clothes he had worn the day of his crowning. In Fay tradition, he was dressed to rule or fade.

The room grew humid as he slumped, the guards grabbing his arms to bolster him. His skin was translucent. Even the clothes he wore grew insubstantial. It seemed he drew strength from them and faltered, losing the last of any potency and will to try and save me. He was near to paying the ultimate price.

I bolted from Aidan's grasping, and ran to his side. "Bring my Father's throne," I ordered.

We settled him as comfortably as possible. He looked into my eyes, speaking like a wisp in the wind. There existed only us.

"Do not weep over me. I am more than ready to meet your mother."

"She said she loves and misses you."

He smiled.

If he wondered how I knew, he gave no indication.

"So Fearghus told the truth. You have returned and are alive and well?"

"But I do not know how much longer that shall last. I fear I have jeopardized my own life."

"You have found true love and consummated it."

I nodded.

"Do you carry proof of such a union within you?"

Again, I nodded. I never believed he would be angry with me, but I began to fear he might. The girl child I had bade care for the deepest part of me, returned. Tears filled our eyes.

"I shall miss not seeing my grandchild. Who is the father? Why do you hesitate? Why not bring him forward and claim him as your King?"

"I fear that is not possible. He is not Fay, but human. I left him behind in the mortal world so I could return home and save my people."

"My sweet daughter, I am sorry to hear that. When the rest of Fay find out, all shall be lost."

I watched his tears of joy turn to misery, and then to anger and alarm. As I touched my Father, I could feel his imminent death consume me, a pain burning and lancing through my heart. Perhaps I would experience many deaths until my own. I was one with the people and my Father. I thought to ask what was wrong, why he seemed so agitated, when the burn within me grew hot and precise.

I turned to see Brigit behind me. She held a dagger sluiced with blood.

My blood.

In the distance, a cry of alarm went up. As the guards lunged to restrain Brigit, she grabbed my hair, and turned to face the room.

"I have overheard the human lover tell her father she carries the babe of a mortal man. This is punishable by death, even for the Princess."

I reached up, pulling my hair from her grasp, and turned to see my father take his last breath. Brigit laughed as the guards whispered of the King's passing, and my legs lost grasp of their duty. Falling to the floor, the cool stones soothed my still heart, and the pain in my back became nothing more than an earthly memory. I tried to focus on the faces above me, but it was no use. The life around me caught against my ethereal skin.

"You will assuredly pay for this," Fearghus growled.

"I'll have your life, too, Fearghus. You have bungled many things. All in my favor, of course."

"Then, you will have my life, also, else I will see to it as another, and another, and another after me surely will."

Jack... I stirred. Jack! Gods, what are you doing here? What about Aine? She is here I know it. My death comes as desolation. Who is with Kyle? Is he forced to die alone?

"Shayla, I am here. Do not leave me."

I opened my eyes. Kyle's warm and misty expression bestowed upon me a final look at life, his eyes twinkling one last time. I sensed my head in his protective lap, cradling me with warmth and tears.

I reached up and grasped at the heart of the blue sweater he wore. "I will never leave you. No one..."

Can take it away.

"Regret..."

Our child would suffer the same fate as we do.

I thought of the alcove above Fearghus' study. My hand and fingers slumped, and I sighed, resigning myself to my fate.

Chapter Eighteen

THE KING CLAIMS HIS BOUNTY

"I am so glad you choose not to fight this, Fay Queen. Do not fear. In mere moments, you shall be mine and suffer no more." Gwyn Ap Nuad appeared as he promised, to claim me upon my deathbed.

No longer the attractive man from the cave, he wore a mantle of horns and teeth, a fearsome creature made of fire and blood. My nostrils flared. I felt myself begin to gag.

"Not kinky? I think myself quite feral and handsome, but loathe not. Even though your dread is quite alluring, when I have your sex, I shall take on a more pleasing form. Stand and take my hand. Fulfill your promise to me. Become my Nether Queen."

I struggled from the ground, realizing I was no longer in the throne room. The walls surrounding me were thick and black with seeping blood, and the rotting stench was overpowering. This was not my beautiful home, but a place of death and torture.

"You will have to do more than change your wretched appearance."

I would do anything to delay my fate. Looking down, I saw my gown was pristine. When I reached around to the back, the warm, life's blood seeping out moments ago, was gone.

White? I would have thought the blood and tragedy more appealing. I had almost asked it aloud. I might not want to know.

"I wished for you to be unscathed, a fresh catch. I savor the taste of blood, and would rather yours to be given freely. I never scavenge off another's jealousies and plotting. Come and take your place where you belong."

"You heal?"

He smirked. "Now you find me desirable."

I looked at the hand held out to me. Encased in earthly skin, there was still a fierce glow beneath.

Here in Gwyn Ap Nuad's realm, he could never completely hide what he was. I was not too sure what to do. Did I have a choice?

"Not too quickly, Death King. She owes me a boon, and our bargain was struck prior to yours. I will have my tribute before you claim her."

I looked up to see the Goddess Aife appear.

Great! They only wanted my death, and neither are willing to allow the other claim. My fate is to spend eternity in limbo, listening to two childish and bickering Deities.

Aife bristled like a cat. "You owed me before him, and I shall take my boon first. I told you your blood would be sweet upon my lips, and the child you yet carry in your womb has not passed. I shall take it to be mine. I have always wanted a child."

My hands drew up to my womb. I would not allow her claim. I turned back to Gwyn Ap Nuad, hoping for his jealousy.

"Will you allow her to take the child? A whole piece of me? Or will you allow the child passage from my body as it should be?"

"What do I care of the thing? I only want you. No child can survive my dwelling. I will not allow it. It is useless to me."

"My child comes before either of you," I shouted. "Unless it is safe, we will be here for an eternity arguing deals, promises made, and promises broken. It is not a part of the bargain."

My choice was to play a third hand, and my anger would not allow me to haggle sanely. Perhaps madness was needed. I did not know the condition of me or my child out of all this. I only knew it would not be a throw-away scrap or plaything.

"Well spoken, Queen Shayla, future of Fay Island. The child is necessary for our people to continue. Neither of these two may make claim. When the time comes, he or she is mine to cull and take my place as the God of Prophecy." Corra smiled.

I clasped my hands tighter. I promised to name a girl child after her, but I knew my baby was a boy. Did the Gods and Goddesses choose whether to pass, and did they choose their children from earth? Stolen from parents as if plucking a flower from a rare plant?

"I challenge thee," Aife shouted. "The babe is mine. She owes me blood, and if fighting you is the only way for me to make claim, then so be it."

No matter how much I wished to side with Corra, who was the best chance, I had my own battle with Gwyn Ap Nuad.

Turning toward him, I reached to my sword.

"You did not believe I would allow a weapon in my Kingdom? No, delicious Queen. You are the prize. I will wait until their battle is done, and then defeat the winner."

"That is not fair. Whoever wins, will be too exhausted to battle you."

"Fair?" His laughter pealed like a bell, as he raised his left hand. "Now. To keep you from interfering."

I advanced, but too late. The wall of glass erected around me, almost causing a bloody nose. I felt the limits of my new cage.

"A curse on you, demon." I could see and hear them, but my voice echoed, resounding eerily. Not being able to yell a warning to Corra bothered me. Gwyn Ap Nuad, perhaps, had a brain. He contained me in fear of something. He understood my love and reason to be my greatest weapons. There was nothing I could do now, except watch as they battled for my life and the life of my son. I knew Corra would win against Aife. Corra had enough worshippers, despite most of Fay beliefs and magic gone astray. It was the reason her cavern was fertile. The other two fed on their hate, fostering dead substance and ineffective worshippers. Corra tended her fruit on love.

Aife hurled a volley of shimmering, psychic blows at Corra. With each splintering rage, she laughed and grew more careless. I knew Corra was the smarter of the two, and I saw her take measure. As Aife wound up for a killing blow, exhausting her powers in one stroke, Corra launched a vast ball of orange light. The comet consumed Aife's icy spears, penetrating toward her heart. The Queen of Shadows had no chance of surviving. She disappeared in a spray of embers.

Gwyn Ap Nuad wasted no time. He raised and aimed his flaming sword at Corra's back, but before he could begin his assault, the weapon was knocked from his hand and tumbled to the ground. My eyes widened as Kyle appeared out of nowhere.

"Watch out!"

Gwyn Ap Nuad turned his fury toward Kyle, choosing to attack him in close quarters with a dagger of molten lead. Kyle blocked each blow, scattering the weapon in a hail of sparks. I would never have believed it, except in a dream walking. Gods battled against each other for the mere sport of it and were many times stronger than mortal man. How was Kyle going to survive?

Tears of helplessness fell down my face. He was going to die, while I could do nothing. This time, I would watch. I realized there had been a steady vibration on the glass, one that had nothing to do with the battle ensuing before me. I turned. Corra was gesturing and concentrating, trying to tell me something. Her lips moved in a strange chanting. I could only hear Gwyn Ap Nuad as he screamed.

Corra moved her hands in a gesture for me to move back. I backtracked as far as the cell would allow, and ducked. The glass vibrated with a soundless tone, growing so intense, I thought my bones would rattle free from my skin. Corra raised her hand and hit the glass hard. The vibration shattered, screaming in my ears as her mallet fell. But what did not fall, was Gwyn Ap Nuad's glass wall.

I turned back to Kyle and saw him, pale and translucent. A large wound had opened near his shoulder that oozed a bright wisp of crimson vapor.

"No..."

I beat upon the walls, slamming my fists and causing the glass to tremble. I did not understand it.

When Corra had struck, the glass had bent into her will, and let it pass through without harm.

When I hit it with my bare hands, it seemed brittle. I felt Corra's power at my back, lending me strength. Not knowing whether the glass would shred my hand into nothingness, I steadied myself and waited before swinging again. I had to time it right. I had to hit the glass at the same time she did.

I sensed her swing, the pitch repeating itself again and again. One swing, and another. At the third, I rammed my fist into the glass.

Pain seared through me, bringing me to my knees. Just as the glass shattered, sending shards deep into my hand, her mallet became my own hand. It struck me. I felt bones splinter, and my hand become a wreck of debris and agony.

I rushed to Kyle just as the Death King swung his final blow, and I triumphed at his shock, as his dagger slammed into my chest. He shimmered for a brief moment, before shrinking completely. The silence was deafening. Gwyn Ap Nuad was gone.

Corra was safe. My son and Kyle's souls were free to pass on.

Kyle held me, running his hand over the wound closing in my chest. Gwyn Ap Nuad's weapons of fire had disappeared with him, and even though the wound had begun to close itself, the damage was done. I felt the festering left there, born of brimstone and perverted fire. The piercing left something deep that would not heal. I was about to die again. At least the Death Deities were not awaiting me this time around. My son may not be born, but he would be safe for all time.

"Help her."

Corra bowed her head. "My love, there is nothing to do. Death in limbo is final."

My body will never fade. I will be forever, laid in deep sleep, never to rise again. This is why so few choose to battle the Gods on their ground.

"I know the tale, sweetheart, but you aren't gone yet. As long as we can keep your eyes opened, we have a chance."

I grew heavy, and I knew I would not wake. I wanted to sleep. I needed to pass away.

"...We do this, she may not be saved and the child lost with or without her."

"I want the child she carries as much as she does, but I want her more. I am willing to live with the consequences. I have lost her too many times in the last few days to survive another. I am living and I am going to live. I refuse to give her up."

"First, I must ask..."

Ask...

I felt myself fade and Kyle yell.

"Now!"

Chapter Nineteen

THE KING AND QUEEN OF FAY REUNITED

I heard weeping and did not understand why. Ask. Nothing. My inner and outer voice seemed years away. Whoever cried, began to scream for help. I tried again, feeling a cloud support me.

Dead.

But clouds were not solid, and stone did not smell of fresh breezes. My fingers pressed against something yielding, as a door slammed and assaulted my ears. My body should be on an altar, not a bed. It was sagging beside me, and a familiar warmth placed itself within my grasp.

Kyle.

Maybe I would dream for eternity, and the dreams would reflect the best memories of my physical life.

"Shayla is waking up. Get Aine. Shayla? Sweetheart? Can you hear me? Squeeze my hand if you can."

He is as real as a dream waking. If I did as he asked, perhaps I could live in reveries with him. But that alternative was not in any tale of Death.

The dead do not stir.

"I came as fast as I could. Jack said she is waking up."

"I thought so, but now I'm not sure. She mumbled something, but hasn't done anything else."

"Give it time, Kyle. She will come back to us."

"It's been three damn months already. How much longer do I have to wait? I can't run this kingdom without her, and I'm tired of going to Fearghus. Even if he did make me King."

His agony broke my heart once more. Why would I dream of his pain? Why did I not dream of him being happy?

"She has not awoken? I had hoped it was true. Aine will have to make more broth."

Now Fearghus appears in my dreams?

"What if we were too late? Corra was sure she was destined to pass. What if she is like this forever?"

"I do not know, son, but if it is true, I believe Corra would give us a sign one way or another. I have been hoping for some intervention."

"It is a sign she breathes."

Jack is back. I giggled and imagined the furrow on my brow to be a deep ravine, capable of sustaining the most interesting of thought creatures. I just needed to sort through them. I plunged into myself.

Maybe I can recreate my last night with Kyle. It is here somewhere.

"What of Brigit and Aidan? What have the Elders decided about them?"

"Brigit is sentenced to eternal exile, and Aidan will go with her. He had a chance, until it was discovered he helped his mother kill Queen Gwendolyn. The Elders hesitated no longer in their decision."

"Exile! I can't believe it. It's not enough. I'm from the mortal world, as you call it, and living there may be hard, but not that hard. Besides, she will no doubt be doing a lot of scheming and damage. She will have an ally in Aidan. They're immortal after all."

"Normally, yes, but the Elders have devised a potion that will force a human life span on them. It should also strip them of any latent powers they may discover or hide. They will not be going to your homeland, but to a deserted island where they will work for everything they need. It is the most the Elders would agree to. Even for killing the Queen."

"And that will work?"

Yes, Kyle. Neither Brigit nor Aidan will last long. If they did find civilization, their true natures would get them into trouble. Fearghus speaks true. Wait! What am I thinking?

None of this was happening.

"She is frowning."

"Shayla!"

"Hello, Father."

His voice rang in my head like a bell, and strength and joy filled me. "Why are you just lying there? Open your eyes and take Kyle's hand to lead your people. Be Queen of Fay with your chosen King by your side. All is now well."

"I must join you, Father. I will greet you in this nether world. You can be my companion. We will find Mother." Again, I tried to open my eyes.

"Nay daughter, it starts with the lights. Go to them. Open your eyes."

"She is awake. Look! Her eyes are opening."

Was Aine also gone from the Fay and in this odd world of the dead? I tried to focus on her, but could not quite see.

"Blink."

I struggled to clear my vision, but there was only grayness with wings floating about me. I needed to pull myself together. I could not live in this limbo, confused and ineffectual forever. I thought to try and use my voice again, and heard a funny hissing. Frustrated, I tried moving my arms.

"So, she does wake. It is all right, my Queen. It will all return in good time. You have been sleeping for over three months now. Your body needs to take care."

I could smell Fearghus' particular scent of spicy bathing oils he preferred.

"Shayla, are you really here? Have you truly returned to me? We have an island to rule, you know."

I blinked in the direction of Kyle's voice, and felt myself being elevated. His heart beat close to mine.

"You are taking her to the waterfall?" Aine asked.

Kyle said it was where we would be together again. Jostled like a newborn in her father's arms, I relaxed my eyes in bliss.

"Hey! You stay awake, you hear me? I need you. Our child needs you."

I nodded.

"Do you think it will work?" Jack asked.

"I was there when the water welcomed her," Aine whispered, "and when they met. If there is any place on Fay that can help, it is the waterfall."

I did not care whether Jack agreed or not. It was tranquil with the falls playing their familiar tune, but there was not the same amount of magical passion as when Kyle and I met.

"The water was silver, and the falls sounded as though they were singing in octaves."

Kyle hesitated. "Well, the water may be normal, but the love I feel for her is the same, if not stronger.

Ever since meeting Shayla, my life has been true and miraculous. I'm going to trust in that."

He walked into the pool, and lowered us to the water's edge. It was warm and comforting, but nothing more. My tears washed with the misty spray and I blinked.

"Trust in me?" Kyle whispered into my hair.

He deserved that much from me, and much more. I nodded and lifted my face up to him.

I love you! Nothing, or no one, can ever take that away from me. Even if I can never see your face again or ever speak the words aloud, I know it. And I know you do, too. That is all that matters.

Could he hear? It did not matter, for with every word I thought, he could see it in my clearing eyes.

"I love you too. May no man or woman break apart what the Deities wrought together."

The water became warmer, and the falls began their song.

Kyle understood, and took us into the depths. As the water swelled about me, I was invigorated, vital and alive. My body trembled in his tender arms. My mind reasoned. At last, there was only one focus and one eternity, and that was Kyle.

I opened my physical eyes to see him smiling down at me, the sparkle in his expression as keen as the day we first met. Raising my hands, I brought his mouth down to mine and kissed him with all the love I had in me. But even though we were once again together, I yet sensed something different.

I reached around to his back, and pulled back my head in shock, nearly choking on the water as my mouth opened to speak. Kyle lifted us to the surface, his chuckle as much music to my ears as the falls.

"I save you from a disreputable God, and you go and drown? There is something not quite right about that."

I stared.

"Do you like them?"

"How?"

"Because I am part Fay, of course."

On his back were a pair of blue Fay wings. I glared at them, then at him. "What do you mean laughing at me? How did you manage to get blue..."

"Are you jealous because they're blue, or is it your need to rid yourself of all the months you have not spoken to me?"

I took a swing at him. My voice. I heard my own Fay voice, and so had he. There was trueness of us, unconcealed in his fine-looking face, his head of thick, black hair, and those twinkling bedroom eyes, the color of midnight blue and silver.

I was healed.

"What else have you grown since I was away?" I asked with a huge grin.

"See? All you needed was faith in me. I hoped one day I would speak the words to you, as you had spoken them to Aine and Jack. All I needed was to believe in you."

The words may not have been exactly the same, but they had come from the heart, and that is all that mattered.

Love. Hate. Fear.

All emotions, whether good or bad, needed to be experienced. For the Fay, it means to be what we were meant to be.

The Most Passionate Creatures of All.

Epilogue
A FUTURE RESTORED

My son was born the 1st of September, and
Goddess Corra graced us with a brief visit, scattering a
few crystals about the baby's crib. I named him after
the most important men in my life. Domhnall
Fearghus Kyle White.

By tradition, we did not use surnames, but it
only seemed right my Mother and Corra should be
honored. Without Mother's wish and Corra's love for
our people, my son would not have existed.

Fearghus took his place as Kyle's great-
grandfather. His Father had named him as the first
O'Connor of the family. And I finally understood.
Fearghus was once a mortal dweller, and had been
one of the men forced to leave a woman he loved
behind. He had suffered knowing his half-human,

half-Fay children were mistreated and labeled cursed in both worlds. He had been eager to change the Law, and hoped I would be the one chosen. When I asked why he had not told Kyle or his family who he was, he said it was better to devise a way to rid the Fay of the Law. He could not bring his children to Fay Island, where he knew they could have magically been saved. Until the Law was abolished, his children would die in either world. Because of an unjust curse, the loss of family would haunt Fearghus forever. I would make sure nothing like it ever happened again.

Kyle and I began our rule the same night. Our first assembly started with Brigit and Aidan's punishment. Neither of us thought being let loose in the mortal world was a good plan, so Kyle devised a jail of sorts, rigged on the island itself. A little something borrowed from Gwyn Ap Nuad.

Even though my Mother had been taken from me, and plans made to murder my Father, I refused to be as cruel. There was only one way in and out of the island, and the door was invisible, moving location on a daily basis. Brigit and Aidan would spend a lifetime trying to find it, and most likely could not do a thing about it anyway. It was an apt thing for too curious minds. Being trapped with each other would be added punishment.

UnKing-like, Kyle hid his laugh by coughing, when we explained it to the Elders. The Elders had smiled. Everything seemed perfect and back in its place.

Aine and Jack expect their first child, and I am pregnant with my second in as many years. We Fay, are truly coming back into ourselves. Our children have become the future once more.

"Shayla, are you coming to bed?" Kyle drawled; it was a deep sexy drawl.

He was planning a wedding anniversary to the new country in America and practiced the accent.

"Oh, yes, my love. I think we shall need to remember how the new babe came to be here." I smiled seductively, encouraging the husky laugh escaping my throat.

He waggled his eyebrows.

"Yes, Mother. A Fay's Wish has come true. Mine!"

The End

Good-Bye, Mother, I will Love and Miss You Always.

Dee

Made in the USA
Columbia, SC
18 September 2021